THE SINS OF SEVEN SERIES

VICE

DANI RENÉ

Published by Dani René

Second Edition Paperback ISBN: 978-1-8384492-5-4

eBook ISBN: 978-0-639-95737-1

WARNING

In a world of secrets, where sins are hidden from sight, people live their lives hoping that those around them never know what desires they conceal. The darkest needs, those that taunt just below the surface. Those they hide in the deepest recesses of their minds. Those things they don't admit to. The things they don't talk about. That's what this series touches on. You may find some of the subject matter disturbing, you may even look away, cringe, and gasp. But that's why I wanted to write these seven couples. These couples came to me with their confessions and I obeyed their need to have their stories told. The dark, depraved, the taboo. The things we may find tempting, alluring, and may even be turned on by it. That's what I wanted to write.

Each story is an interconnected standalone, delving into the relationship of the couples you'll meet. There will be sex, there will most certainly be foul language. And there will DEFINITELY be taboo subjects covered.

The Sins of Seven revolves around seven couples who are so different in nature, in what their likes and dislikes are. They're each unique in desire, in their personalities, and even in the way they try to show affection. They don't love. At least, they don't think they do, they don't believe they're worthy of it.

Each story will make a point of focusing on one of the seven deadly sins.

Greed, Pride, Lust, Gluttony, Sloth, Wrath, Envy.

Although they'll be released in their own order, you'll be able to tell which sin, follows which couple and their journey to possibly find their happily ever after.

Please heed this warning.

**This is a dark romance, suitable for mature audiences, 18+ ONLY. Strong sexual themes and violence, which could trigger emotional distress, are found in this story. Certain scenes are graphic and could be upsetting to some. This story is NOT for everyone. Proceed with caution. Discretion is advised.*

Dedication

Since Oliver first appeared in Kneel, book one of the series, there have been two ladies who've without a doubt fought for him. This is for you Allyson and Anna. I guess you'll have to share him!

Dani xo

PLAYLIST

Desire - Meg Myers

Black Widow - Iggy Azalea, Rita Ora

The After You - Miakoda

Unsteady - X Ambassadors

Low Life - Future, The Weeknd

In the Night - The Weeknd

Love Faces - Tre Songz

Silhouette - Birdy

Monster - Meg Myers

My way - Tom Walker

Walk Through The Fire - Mary Gauthier

Find the full playlist on Spotify

Sloth is the vilest of sins.

Laziness will destroy you if you allow it.

Unknown

PROLOGUE

OLIVER

There was never a time I can recall that I didn't derive my pleasure from pain.

Since I was in my late teens, the act of pain brought pleasure. At the time I thought I was broken. I believed my desires had been altered, and there was no hope for me. I ignored it. Shoved it into the recesses of my mind because I knew it was wrong.

Pleasure and pain could not coincide.

Every day, I went through my routine of school, work, and chores. When I finally moved out of my childhood home and into the dorms where I studied at Northwestern, I found my calling. Not one of those epiphanies where you realize you need God or some fucked-up religion. No, I found my calling as a Master, which I'm now known as.

At first, I was unsure of this life, but as I played out scene after scene, I knew it was what I needed to push my past behind me and move forward.

God was never there for me, so I didn't expect him to answer, even if I prayed. I focused on what came naturally to me, and I realize that all this time, I was only doing what I was meant to all along.

As a Master, I'm here to train inexperienced men and women who know something is missing in their lives, and to show them the *other* way.

The leather, ropes, metal cuffs, and chains, those are the instruments I use to ensure that those who kneel before me find pleasure in the pain I inflict.

For those who aren't familiar with the lifestyle, I'm called a sadist.

The people who kneel and bow for me are known as masochists.

And we find pleasure in the darkness of BDSM. Yes, there are many fetishes, and we each have our own way of finding bliss. Euphoria.

The room I walk into is dark, with only the dim light

of candles I've set out illuminating the space. Golden shimmers of flames dance along the red walls. I'm wearing a black suit, crisp, white dress shirt, and a pair of shiny black Oxfords. I've just come from the office where I've had a meeting with Nathan Ashcroft, one of my best friends, and a Dominant, like me.

On the floor before me is a beautiful blonde woman. At thirty-seven, she's one of the older submissives I train. Her curves are voluptuous, her tits heavy with dark brown nipples that are extremely sensitive. Her skin is smooth, tanned, and beautiful to the eye.

"Eyes up," I order, commanding her with two words.

She lifts her blue eyes, meeting mine with a shy, sultry gaze.

"Have you been a good girl for me?" I question, shrugging off my jacket, hanging it on the back of the chair.

"Yes, Sir," she says, addressing me the way I taught hcr.

Each woman who walks in here has rules. I'm not a Master to all, and I'm not a sadist with everyone. They each have their own wants and needs, and I fulfill those as best I can.

I have a waiting list of men and women vying for the next spot in my dungeon.

I've never believed in owning one slave. Never allowed myself to give a collar to one woman or man. The variety I'm afforded is what I crave. Seeing beautiful bodies at my mercy every day is something I've become accustomed to.

"Spread your legs," I command, while my shirt finds its spot atop my jacket. Next are my shoes. Placing them neatly beneath the chair, I pad over to her. She's facing the door, her body nude, hands on her thighs, palms up. Her are legs wide, offering me a view of her pussy.

I scrutinize her for a moment, stalking around her. There's a slight tremor in her body, and I wonder if she's wet already.

"You didn't shave."

It's an observation. She doesn't need to respond, which she doesn't. I can't help my satisfied smile, she's learning. When I reach her front, I crouch to face her.

"What is it you want, Misty?" I question.

"To be owned by a Master," she responds easily.

"And do you think he'll enjoy eating your hairy cunt?"

She blushes at my use of words. "No, Sir."

"Exactly. I want you to go to the bathroom, bring everything you'll need to shave, and I'll watch you."

She gapes at my order but knows better than to question me. Slowly, she rises, perfectly poised for what she'll soon have to endure. Not all men are like me. Some prefer hair, others not. Me? I'm meticulous, and every woman who walks out of here is clean, smooth, and ready to be devoured.

I never love them.

I never allow myself to feel.

And I never let my cock make my decisions.

I'm cold, I'm calculated, and I'm far from someone you want to love.

That's an emotion I no longer possess.

It's been a long time since I allowed myself to love someone. And when I did, my heart was torn from my chest with vicious claws. That's why I no longer seek a long-term playmate. My role as a sadist revolves around the pleasure I derive from training and delving out the pain. It's all I need in my life these days.

Don't get me wrong. I fuck.

Hard. Rough. Violent.

The only time I've found my utmost pleasure is when a slave is on his or her knees crying, begging for mercy, blood dripping from their beautiful flesh — beautiful flesh I've marred with my whip or cane.

I'm the ultimate monster.

And you do not want to get into the cage with me.

OLIVER

Stalking through my office building—Michaelson and Associates—I head to the elevators which will take me to my office which is situated on the top floor. I ignore the pretty little brunettes who run after me with messages and calls I've missed.

I'm angry.

So fucking livid I could easily take one of them into my office and spank her until she's red, raw, and whimpering. I need to see blushing flesh below me. Beneath me. When I take a quick glance around the reception area, I notice Lori standing idly behind the desk.

"Lori," I bark, my voice carrying over the people waiting to see me. She leaps into the air, her eyes darting my way in shock and fear. "In my office. Now." Ignoring everyone else, I make my way up the stairs, taking them two at a time. If I tire myself out, I'll go easy on her.

Who am I kidding?

I never go easy on any of the toys who enter my chambers.

When I step inside, I inhale a deep, cleansing breath, hoping it will calm me down. But when the beautiful, dark-haired vixen walks in, my body is once again on full alert.

"Hike your skirt up over your waist, and bend over my desk. Now."

She gapes at me for a second, but when I pin her with a glare, she jumps into action. Not questioning me, just obeying. Most of the women who work for me are submissive. They may not play within the lifestyle, but their personalities are shy and obedient.

That's why I do all the interviews for my staff. No Human Resources department will know what I'm looking for, and they won't find the gems hidden within the dust.

Some of the women who do walk in here know who

I am from Seven Sins, and they beg me for this life, so I give it to them. I allow them into my world, because I realized a long while ago, once you've tasted the forbidden fruit, there's no hiding the hunger for it.

Pulling my belt from the loops, I twist it around my hand, gripping the thick leather in a fist. The beautiful curve of her ass is perfectly poised to receive a harsh swat. Lifting my arm, I bring it down on her flesh.

She cries out, and my dick throbs while an angry red welt turns her pretty creamy skin a shade I've come to revel in. I land another sweet sting on her behind, the pattern blushing like a piece of artwork.

"Oli." My best friend's voice comes from behind me. When I turn to find Nathan Ashcroft at the entrance of my office, I drop the belt and pull Lori up. "Was I interrupting?" he smirks, shutting the door behind him and stalking closer.

"Not at all. Lori was learning why she should listen to me when I explain something," I inform him easily. Reaching between her thighs, I press a finger to her cunt, finding it drenched and slick.

"I'm sorry, Daddy," she coos, her fat bottom lip

trembling. She's been my assistant for three years. Her body has been bent in every position in this damn office. "I didn't mean to be a bad girl." Her sweet, innocent voice only serves to harden my cock. I'd love to fuck her right now, but I have things to do.

"You should be. Now go to your desk, and do not use a pillow under your ass. I want you to flinch when you sit down."

She doesn't respond, merely scurries out of my office, her head stooped and her eyes on the floor. Nate chuckles as he settles himself in the black leather chair opposite my desk.

"You're still a harsh asshole, I see," he utters with amusement in his voice.

I've known Nathan for many years. When we met at college, there was an immediate connection between us. His snarky attitude and confident demeanor matched my own, and even now, years later, he's my closest friend.

When we started training together, both of us focused on becoming Dominants, and we learned how to use anger for pleasure, or never walk into a BDSM club again. Needless to say, we took to it like a fish to water.

His need for humiliation stems from his younger years, growing up with a father who would prefer to degrade him in front of his friends, girlfriends, anyone who he brought into their home. Years of that took its toll on the young mind, and since then, he's been the one to dole it out. Only now, he has Eva who enjoys it, who challenges him, but what I taught him was to hone that need into this dark world we live in.

Not all slaves or submissives can handle it. Some flinch at the words cunt or slut, but the beautiful Eva is the light in Nate's dark. She takes it and devours it. She drinks in everything he gives and begs for more.

"To what do I owe this pleasure, old friend?" I settle myself in the chair behind my desk, meeting Nate's dark eyes.

"I was in town and thought I'd see how you're doing. The club on the West Coast is really taking off, so I needed to meet with Rick and Mason," he smirks happily. There's never been a time I wasn't proud of Nathan. He's made a name for himself, picking up the pieces of his life and building something utterly beautiful.

"I've been busy. Rick has submissives lining up out the door for me to train. However," — I lean forward, my forearms resting on my desk — "his sister has been begging me to train her." I inform him of the newest little pet I've been hankering after. Her pert ass is just beautiful, and I can't wait to see her poised, kneeling, and even spreading her body for me.

"Carrick's sister?" Nate's brows shoot up, surprise written all over his face. "And he's okay with that?" Nathan knows Carrick as well as I do, and as much as he's against his sister joining the world of BDSM, that's not his choice to make, and Carrick knows it.

"Not exactly; however, if a submissive wants to train, I'm not one to deny her," I tell him, shrugging my shoulders. And Nathan knows I'm right.

Nate nods, mulling it over in his mind. "That's true. I've only met her once, but she seems lovely."

"She is. Sweet, innocent, and so new to all this that it's refreshing." I can't help smiling when I think of Cayleigh. She's eager to learn, but there's also this shyness to her that makes my dick harder than it's ever been. "How are Eva and the kids?"

"She's doing really well. Ainsley and Allyson are growing up far too quickly," he informs me with a glint of happiness in his dark gaze. Love does strange things to people, but it's made Nate a man who no longer dwells on the past. He's forgiven his father and mother for their part in his upbringing, and he's now showing his kids how a father should be. When I heard about his childhood, rage fueled me into finding the asshole. I made sure Nathan's father couldn't see straight when I finished with him.

"When are they going to visit? I think Uncle Oliver needs to spend some time around the little munchkins."

He chuckles at my request before responding with a smile. "You know, Oliver, in all the years I've known you, I would never have thought I'd hear you say the word *munchkins.*"

"Life is full of surprises, Nathan."

"I'll bring them the next time I'm out. We're thinking of coming for a Thanksgiving vacation." He nods, rising from his chair. "I'm heading to see Rick. I'll see you tonight?"

"Yes, I'll be meeting with Cayleigh."

"Great." I watch him saunter from my office, the door ajar, and I catch a glimpse of my assistant who's eye-fucking Nathan like she's a starving woman. That's the effect he has on most women.

Shaking my head, I pull out my phone and find the number I've been avoiding, not because I don't want to call him, but because I know he'll want a scene.

Peyton's brother, Chance, has been begging to learn from me. He's what they call a switch. He's told me he wants to be a submissive for me, but I've noticed how he enjoys dominating women, and I'm thinking about taking both him and Cayleigh on to see how they fair in this world.

Hitting dial, I lean back, planning the next thirty days in my mind.

CAYLEIGH

It's been a long while since I've felt wanted, needed. My brothers and father are strict, and since I lost the one man I had pledged my life to, I've been on a spiral. There's no going back from watching the man you love get murdered in cold blood while standing beside you at the altar.

Glancing at myself in the mirror, I take in the way the blue silk dress hugs my curves. My breasts aren't huge, but the bra I'm wearing pushes them up, offering a hint of cleavage, which I'm hoping will impress Oliver.

The older man has been on my mind daily since we met. I've begged him to train me, to teach me the lifestyle my brothers seem so enamored with. Tonight, Oliver has agreed to take me into one of the rooms for a scene.

I've never done anything like this before, and my nerves are frayed as I slip on the silver sandals I bought earlier. I've opted for light makeup, which isn't too drastic in color but offers a dark line allowing my eyes to pop. My hair is styled in a messy bun with strands to frame my face.

Inhaling a deep, calming breath, I make my way out of the apartment Carrick has gifted me. Living upstairs from the club isn't my first choice, but for now, I let my older brother look after me in his own possessive way.

When I reach the club floor, I find the space filled with people. It's only seven in the evening, but all the tables are filled with clients. A man steps away from the bar, allowing me to step closer and order a drink from Dylan who offers me a wink.

He sets the glass of white wine in front of me, giving me his signature smile. He's cute, but for some reason, I can't find it in myself to want him. He asked me on a date the first week I arrived in Chicago from London, but as much as I'd like to go on a normal date, I know I'd be bored.

The men who prefer their vanilla tastes tend to

frustrate me. There's a sweetness, gentleness to them, and it's not something that interests me. I want darkness and danger. When I was with Sean, he was everything I craved —rough, violent, and rugged.

Each man who came afterward was merely there to allow me to forget the pain. The violence I came to know all my life stole Sean from me, and I knew I'd never be the same. Hence the reason I'm here. Wanting something more.

Something else has captured my attention, and it's in the form of an older man who has been on my mind for months now. Even though Carrick doesn't approve of me taking a step into this world, I can't stop myself.

"There she is." The deep, sensual voice of Oliver skitters over my bared skin. The thin straps of my dress slink over my shoulders, offering a view of my arms and neck, allowing his warm breath to send tingles straight to my core.

"Hello, Oliver." I smile when he sidles up beside me. He seats himself on the bar stool and watches me for a moment before lifting his hand to signal for a drink. Dylan doesn't need to hear what he wants. The tumbler is set before the man without question.

"How is the lovely Irish princess?"

"I'm very well," I respond, offering a shy smile. There's something about Oliver Michaelson that makes my body thrum, but it also makes me nervous. I haven't ever delved into the dark, taboo scenes he's played out, but I've seen one or two, and it's intrigued me. I know he's the only man who can dole out the one fantasy I've always been too scared to ask for.

"Would you like to play a scene this evening? It will be with Chance and me." He lifts the glass to his lips, making my gaze track the movement as he sips the amber liquid. Dressed in a pastel blue shirt with a dark-colored tie, it makes his tanned skin and salt-and-pepper hair look even more distinguished than ever before.

"Yes, please." I nod, offering him another big grin.

When Oliver smirks, I have to squeeze my thighs together. There's a sinfulness to him that makes my stomach tumble with anticipation.

Chance appears in the doorway to the club. Catching my gaze, he smiles as he nears us with a confident stroll. "Sweet Cay," he greets me, pressing his lips to my cheek.

"Oliver." The men shake hands easily as if they've been friends for years, but I know Chance has a crush on the older man. I don't blame him.

"Cayleigh will be joining us this evening," Oliver informs Chance.

"I look forward to it." The green-eyed young man smiles. He looks just like his sister, Peyton, who married Carrick, my brother, two years ago, and now have a beautiful family. I didn't think my brother would ever get over the loss of his fiancée, but thankfully, Peyton has made him see reason. The family he now has definitely changed him from a man-whore to a dad who seems to be wrapped around both daughters' fingers. They're his princesses, and I know he'd do anything for them.

"Shall we?" Oliver offers as he rises, buttoning his suit jacket. I nod, following him farther into the back of the club with Chance hot on my heels.

I know Oliver has a list of women and men all vying for his attention, and I'm thankful he's decided to take us on as trainees. To guide us through this lifestyle and show us just what it entails.

There have been whispers about Oliver being bi,

and I've seen him chatting to men and women, taking them into the playrooms, but I've never actually seen him engage in a sexual act with both sexes at the same time.

I suppose there's always a first for everything.

OLIVER

As we all enter the room, Chance shuts the door behind him, while Cayleigh strolls around the space, taking it in with wide eyes. I settle in the armchair, resting my ankle over the opposite knee, watching their inquisitive nature take hold.

"This is incredible," Cayleigh murmurs. She trails her fingertips over the leather of a flogger hanging against one wall. A small shiver trickles through her, making the need to adjust my cock. I've been sweet and romantic to certain submissives, but there are times I prefer being a sadist, whipping porcelain flesh until it's bright red with welts.

"So, we're doing this together?" Chance questions.

"If you want to do this correctly, then we'll talk

before getting into the scene," I tell them, gesturing to the chairs positioned close to where I'm seated. The room itself has somewhat of a lounge area with seating and a small table. I've used the table before, but definitely not for drinks.

Once they're both seated, I take them in for a moment. Laying eyes on Cayleigh, the sweet, innocent Irish girl with big hazel eyes, then Chance, the boy who's intrigued me since he walked into the club. His sister is one of the most beautiful women in Sins; however, Carrick has already laid claim to her, sadly.

"I'll train you both. I've decided to take Chance's switch tendencies and see how he reacts to you in a scene," I tell Cayleigh. Then dragging my gaze over to the young man, I offer, "And you'll learn from me how to dominate, as well as learning to submit."

"And after?" This comes from the sweet girl. As much as I'd like to offer them more, I don't. That's not who I am as there has never been a submissive I've wanted to collar, to keep around after our thirty-day training sessions.

"Afterwards, you find a Dom or Domme, depending

on your proclivities, and you'll embark on a relationship that will suit you."

"How would I know what suits me?" Once again, a curious kitten.

"You'll learn from me. We'll take it slow, ease into this lifestyle. With each scene, I'll test your limits. We'll see how far you're willing to bend, how much pain you're able to handle, and ultimately, you'll learn what it is you need. Deep down," I tell them. "This isn't about dating, or marriage, or any of those mundane acts. Being in this lifestyle is deeper. It speaks to your soul. Once you find someone you're able to connect with on that level, you'll find it's so much more than just a spanking, or blindfold, or any of that other shit you read about in books."

"I want this," Chance says easily without hesitation. I knew he would. He's eager to learn. He's beautiful to look at, and I'm certain he has a cock that will have men and women on their knees wanting to worship it.

"Me too," Cayleigh agrees. There's a soft redness to her cheeks, a blush that makes my dick hard.

Nodding, I gesture to Chance. "You've sent me your

tests. Thank you." Glancing at Cayleigh, I question, "And you? Have you gotten yours done?"

"Yes, I have them here." She smiles. Opening her purse, she fishes out the envelope and hands it to me. I don't need to look at it because I know she's clean. The doctor I sent them both to is one of my good friends, but they don't need to know that. Not yet anyway.

Living in Chicago, I have numerous contacts, and with the work I've done over the years for each of those men, they owe me their lives and their livelihoods. And if I need information on a new sub, I can get it with one phone call or email.

"The contracts will be drawn up and sent to you via email. You'll both read through them extensively, familiarize yourself with each point, and we'll discuss your hard limits. Most people have them, and I'd be surprised if you told me you don't."

"I thought we were going to do a scene tonight?" Chance questions, his brows furrowing and those green eyes glittering like they have stars in them.

"Oh, we are," I smirk. Rising from my chair, I reach for Cayleigh and tug her to standing. "I want to see how well you take orders tonight. There won't be any intercourse or intense scenes played out until I have those signed contracts and your list of limits. Then we delve into more."

I lead Cayleigh over to the chair I was sitting on. Positioning her to face away from Chance and me, I move behind her while inhaling her sweet scent as I gently move the stray strands of her hair. The deep brown of her locks reminds me of chocolate. I've seen them loose, and her tresses are the perfect length to wrap around my hand while controlling her movement.

"I'm going to take your dress off now, Cayleigh," I tell her, lowering my tone so it's merely a whisper against her cheek. "If at any point you're uncomfortable, or find you're reaching your limit tonight, you have a safe word. Red is stop, and yellow will let me know you're nearing your limit but want more. Do you understand?"

She nods, a small smile on her full, pinkish lips. "Yes, Oliver." Her voice is gentle, like a stream trickling over pebbles. It's calming, and I find myself intrigued by the exquisite, innocent woman.

"You will address me as Sir while we're in this

room."

"Yes, Sir."

Reaching for her zipper, I gently pull it down until I reach the arch at her lower back, then nudge the material over her shoulders, allowing the dress to fall and pool at her feet. She's dressed in black and blue. The lace corset along with her panties are dark with bright blue ribbons snaking from top to bottom. It's exquisite.

"You look beautiful, Cayleigh," I tell her, admiring her curves as I step back and allow my gaze to drink her in. She has a small tattoo on her thigh, a Claddagh sign which I recognize instantly, causing my heart to ache in my chest.

The Irish symbol is a reminder of a past I'd rather forget, but I've agreed to do this, so I can't walk away from her now. There was once a boy I'd wanted more than anyone, and he used to wear the symbol on a chain around his neck. He told me his father being Irish gave it to him before he died. He treasured the piece of metal. Shaking my head, I shove the memories from my mind and focus on the girl in front of me.

"I want you to kneel on the chair, hold the backrest,

and don't look behind you. This is a test of your obedience," I tell her.

Silently, she obeys, positioning her knees on the cushion, her head remaining still as she faces the window looking out over the club. Even though the people on the other side can't see us, I find it erotic knowing there is a possibility of someone watching, a voyeur getting off on what I'm about to do.

"Chance," I call to the young man who's on his feet in seconds. "I want you to take the crop, and we'll see how much Cayleigh enjoys a spanking with the implement."

He nods, reaching for the long object with a small leather patch at the end, which offers a small sting I find most new subs enjoy.

"Cayleigh, I want you to count. Chance, I want you to alternate with your spanks."

He nods. Raising the crop, he brings it down on the pert ass cheek of Cayleigh who whimpers, then counts as I ordered. They continue while I observe. Chance is gentle at first, but when they reach twelve, I notice he's getting comfortable with what he's doing.

"Stop."

He halts the moment the word falls from my lips. Gripping Cayleigh's panties, I slide them over her hips and leave them at her thighs. Her ass is pink with small shapes from the crop, and my dick jolts at the sight. It's beautiful seeing porcelain skin darken with a soft blush.

"Cayleigh, you're rather lovely." I gesture to Chance, showing him how to massage her body where he's inflicted the pain. Watching them together is sensual. There's something sweet and innocent about it, but I have a feeling as we venture into the more difficult kinks, they'll both bask in it. Just watching Chance's eyes shimmer with need as he continues his actions reminded me of myself when I was his age.

"Please," Cayleigh whimpers suddenly.

"Speak, pet," I tell her, my voice deep and commanding.

"I . . . I need to come." Her voice cracks. The huskiness is evidence she enjoyed her spanking, and that only makes me want to take it a step further.

"Do you want to see what I would do to you once you're used to this?" My question is aimed at both of them but more to Cayleigh.

"Yes, Sir."

Stalking to the wall, I pick up the phone which dials out to the bar area. I hit dial and wait. Once Dylan answers, I ask for the one woman I've always enjoyed when I've walked into Seven Sins. "Send Willow into the black room," I tell him and hang up.

I don't have to wait long before the door clicks and in walks the redhead. She's tall, dressed in a long, bright red dress that hits the floor. Her long hair hangs in fiery waves down her back.

"I'd like to play with you while they watch," I tell her.

"Yes, of course, Sir." She smiles in agreement. Before I have time to order her to undress, she's already taken the initiative and stepped out of her gown.

The tiny red thong she's wearing is all that's under the silky material, and I'm even harder seeing her tits with those perky nipples peaked and ready for attention. I plan to see how turned on my two newbies get while watching me.

"I want you both on these chairs," I tell Cayleigh,

who's trembling with need to come. Edging a sub is always an erotic experience, and I can't wait to see how much I can torture Cayleigh and Chance with it, but I want them to witness first-hand a short scene.

CHANCE

Granted, I've had a crush on the man since I first saw him, and I can't deny I want him to collar me. I've wanted it for a while now, and I don't know how I'll ever find someone to match my needs other than him.

He doesn't know I've researched him. He also doesn't know how much I've stalked him over the past months since we met. It may be wrong, but I needed to know who he is, under the suit of armor he usually wears.

There's nothing about him online. The tidbits of information I did find didn't quench my thirst for more, and now as I watch him with this woman, it only solidifies how much I crave him.

Oliver is more than handsome. He's every girl's

dream man and every guy's wet dream come true. The moment I saw him, I knew I wanted him. When he finally agreed to train me, I wasn't sure how I would cope with the scenes, but with this introduction to what we have in store for us, I know I'll love every moment.

Cayleigh is stunning. Her body is a perfect hourglass, which makes my cock rock hard, and watching her pert little ass turn a shade of rosy pink has only ensured that we'll indeed enjoy our training more than we both expected.

I want to taste her. I want Oliver to fuck me while I do, but right now, I'm intrigued as to what he has planned for us with the redhead who walked in.

Cayleigh and I are seated, watching as Oliver has the woman kneel in the same spot Cayleigh was in moments ago. Her body is beautiful, and I can't help wondering how a foursome between us would feel. An experience I'll be new to, but one I'd love nonetheless.

"Get on the bed, pet. It's time for our scene," Oliver commands in a calm, controlled tone, and I wonder how he's holding himself together. I'm so hard I could cut glass with my dick.

Oliver turns the sound system on, which plays a soft classical song I don't recognize. He smirks over at us as he grabs the flogger from the hook against the wall.

"One of my favorite implements," he tells us, then proceeds to whip the woman who's whimpering, but her control is astounding because anyone else would've been screaming. "See how quiet she's being? Just tiny mewls of pleasure that trickle through her and tumble from her lips." Oliver smiles. "That's a well-trained sub, knowing how I prefer it. If you want to speak, you need to ask for permission." He talks to us but continues his sensual torture of the redhead.

When he finally drops the flogger, he gently pulls Willow's panties down.

"Open your legs," he orders her, his tone changing as he takes on his Dominant persona. She obeys without a word. There's something deeply sensual about her obedience. That's what turns me on, but I don't know if I could ever be as dominant as Oliver is.

He crouches down, running his hands along her thighs. Spreading her open, he leans in and slowly inhales her. A smirk on his lips confirms she's wet, ready for him.

"The Dominant you find will either offer pleasure, or he'll deliver punishment. It depends on the situation and what's happened between you both that day, before the scene." His voice is husky, raspy, and I am tempted to touch myself.

"Sir," Willow finally utters.

"Speak."

"I'm wet. So very wet." Her voice is a mere whisper, but we all hear it.

"Good girl," Oliver coos. Unbidden jealousy rages through me at the thought of him wanting her and not me.

"Such a pretty cunt," he observes, pulling a thick leather belt from his loops. Without warning, he brings it down on her thighs, first the left, then the right. I've never watched him in action, and I find myself hard as a fucking rock.

My cock throbs when he palms his dick in his slacks. The welts that rise up on Willow's flesh are beautiful, and the way she's whimpering and shivering tells me she loves them too. My body is ready to bow for him, to bend over and take anything he has to offer.

Steel gray eyes meet mine. Oliver Michaelson is not a man; he's a God. Thunder and lightning shimmer in his gaze. Those orbs that remind me of a storm turn dark as he regards me.

"Come here, Chance," he orders, and I'm already on my feet, closing the distance between us. When I reach him, he grips my shirt, tugging me closer. His lips whisper over mine, causing my dick to respond with a jolt. "Do you like watching me whip her pretty cunt?"

"I do, Oliver."

"Good," he smirks, dropping his hand to my bulge, gripping my shaft through the material. His hold on me is breathtaking because I know if I move even an inch, he'll cause me severe pain. But something tells me that's not what he wants to do.

"Sir," Willow whimpers from the bed, but he doesn't turn to her.

"Get on all fours," he commands her, but his gaze and grip are on me. He massages my dick, eliciting a groan from me. "Take my dick out." This time I'm unsure as to who he's speaking to because I'd gladly take him out. But Willow moves quickly. Once her tiny hand wraps around his thick shaft, his eyes flutter, and for a moment, I see him. Not the sadist, but the man.

"May I suck your cock, Sir?" Willow questions in a low tone, but he raises his hand to the back of my head and pushes me to my knees.

"Chance is going to share with you," he tells her, then flits his gaze to Cayleigh who's staring wide-eyed at the scene before her. "And you, my lovely little Irish princess," he smirks at her, "will eat Willow's pretty pussy."

Cayleigh moves with confidence. Her kneeling on the mattress is stunning. I've been with a handful of women before, but she's breathtaking. Perhaps it's her submissiveness, or maybe it's how she blushes with knowing what she's about to do, but all I want to see is her mouth wet with arousal.

I finally get a grip on Oliver's cock and gently stroke him. Willow watches me intently, mesmerized at my movements as she smiles. My tongue darts out, lapping at the tip of his erection, tasting the salty flavor of his desire for us.

His hand tangles in my hair, gripping the strands as our gazes lock. "Suck me until I feed you my seed," he grunts, allowing me to suck him deep into my mouth, feeling the tip hit the back of my throat.

My movements allow Willow to lean in and suckle on his heavy sac, her mouth enveloping them. Her cheeks sink in as she works. Cayleigh's face disappears as Willow's moans echo around us, and I know the intoxicating girl is already enjoying herself.

Oliver's hips move faster as he fucks my face, and I allow it. I want him to lose control. To see a man like him lost in pleasure is erotic in itself. His grip in my hair tightens, and I feel his cock throb and thicken. With a growl, his hips jerk wildly, and my mouth is filled with hot jets of arousal.

The saltiness hits my tongue, and I hold it in my mouth until he pulls from between my lips. He watches in awe when I pull Willow toward me, sharing the white seed with her. Leaning in, I kiss her, our tongues dance as she cries out as her orgasm rips through her, causing her to shiver in my arms.

Cayleigh rises from the bed, kneeling beside me,

and I turn to her. She smiles as she presses a shy kiss to my lips, which I only deepen when I pull her closer. We all share Oliver's release as we kiss and lick at each other.

I'm still hard, still needy for an orgasm when the man who brought us together growls in a husky drawl, "Chance." My name on his lips sounds like a beautiful symphony. When I meet his gaze, he smirks wolfishly. "Fuck Cayleigh. I want to watch."

He doesn't need to ask me twice. Lifting the beautiful woman, I help her back onto the mattress. My cock is out seconds later as Willow grips my shaft in her delicate hand and strokes me twice before positioning me at Cayleigh's sweet little cunt. Without another thought, I slide into the tightest hole I've felt in a long time. My hips move of their own accord as I pull out and slam back in. Again and again.

My eyes roll back, and I'm lost in pleasure as I feel hands gripping my ass. I know it's Willow, but I don't stop fucking Cayleigh. She leans in and slowly licks along my shaft, causing me to grunt and slam harder into the pretty girl who's staring up at me with the most beautiful eyes.

Willow's mouth is magic against the tight ring of muscle as she tongues me, and Cayleigh's pussy is perfection. I'm lost once more to the need and desire driving through me at an alarming rate. The sound of skin slapping, grunting, and groaning are the only echoes I hear as Cayleigh moans as her body arches when her orgasm rocks through her, and her walls pulse around me, milking me.

"That's it, baby girl." I lean in as Willow pushes two fingers into my ass, finger-fucking me fast and deep. It doesn't take long for me to empty myself inside Cayleigh, and soon I'm coming down from a high I've never once experienced.

"Perfect," Oliver observes from the chair in the corner where I was seated earlier. He's dressed as if he'd never had his cock out or even had his shirt unbuttoned. I wonder briefly if this man ever gets ruffled. Is there ever a moment he unleashes himself from the tight reigns he has?

"Oliver—"

"You may go, Willow," he informs our guest with a

wave of his hand. Once we're alone, he looks over at my sweet girl and me. "You two will be perfection." He nods as he rises. "Get dressed. Tomorrow, we'll do something special. Thank you for a rather enlightening scene," he tells us before leaving the room and shutting the door behind him.

"He's strange," Cayleigh tells me.

"He is, but he's the best," I agree, but deep down, my chest aches because as much as I want this, want Oliver to train us, I also want to delve into the darkness he hides and see what's hurting him so much.

"I guess we can have a drink now."

"That we can, sweet girl," I tell her. "That we can."

CAYLEIGH

Rolling over, I stare at the ceiling with my body still buzzing from the scene last night. As much as I enjoyed it, I can see that Oliver is more of a mentor to me. He will prepare me for the day I find the Dominant who can offer me a future.

Oliver has intriguing kinks. His needs are what I would love to offer him as a submissive, but I realize for myself this is merely learning. At first, I thought I'd want to be his, but with every moment I've spent with him, I know he and Chance are suited perfectly. If only Oliver could admit it.

One thing I did notice is the man is closed off. He's shut himself away from every emotion other than the scenes he plays. Which begs the question — what happened to him? Nobody shuts down like that unless they've had their heart broken in some way.

I may be young, but I've lived through pain. I still do. Every day is a challenge. Though I've found solace in the BDSM community, spending time at Seven Sins has offered me a place where I can explore safely.

And I know I want more.

Yes, I want to be a submissive, but I want a man who will have eyes only for me. Even though I care for Chance, I know I could never be in a relationship with two other hearts.

I wonder then where this leaves me. Oliver said he'd train me for a Dominant, and I'm welcome to find someone who'll give me what I need when I feel ready for it. There's something about Oliver always being there for everyone, but what makes my chest ache is that he's never found a forever for himself. And deep down, I hope he can find that with Chance.

After last night, I came home and dreamt about Sean. He was there, offering me his hand, smiling, and I hope it meant he's happy I'm finally moving on from the pain of our past. My mind is a mess. I don't know how or what to think.

Picking up my phone, I hit dial on Oliver's number. Pressing the device to my ear, I wait for his deep rumbling tone to come over the line.

"Cayleigh." He utters my name with admiration and affection, which makes my heart flutter wildly in my chest.

"I'd like to talk."

"My office is always open to you. Come over at one, and we can sit down and discuss," he tells me, and I can hear the smile in his voice. I wonder if he knew I'd be calling him.

"I'd like that. Thank you, Oliver," I respond with a grin. There's something about his caring demeanor that he doesn't offer just to anyone, and I wonder if he does it because Carrick is my brother.

"I look forward to it. Just don't wear panties," he orders, then hangs up without another word. My tummy tumbles with excitement at what he has in store for me.

When I enter the offices of Michaelson and

Associates, I take in the elegant surroundings. Rather than the modern, clean lines I'm expecting, the darker colors of a deep cabernet along with charcoal line the walls. The furniture is black leather, with ornate mahogany desks, and I can't help finding the richness of the space rather intriguing. It's strange seeing an office decked out this way, and even though it's unique, it works, and somehow fits Oliver's personality to a T.

I know Oliver works with lawyers, but I'm not sure if he goes into court. But then again, I know he and my brother Callan have done some undercover work in the past as well. So, to be honest, I have no idea what the man does.

"Good afternoon." A gentle female voice drags me from my thoughts, and my gaze finds hers. She's young, probably my age, and utterly beautiful. She reminds me of a painting rather than a real woman.

"Hello, I'm here to see Mr. Michaelson," I tell her.

The woman nods as if she were the one expecting me. She rises from her seat, rounding the desk, and nearing me, she offers a hand. "I'm Gennie. Nice to meet you."

"Likewise," I smile.

"This way. He's in his office." She turns and heads toward two large oak doors down a short hallway. As we make our way, the only sound that's made is the clacking of our heels on the rich wooden floor.

Gennie taps her knuckles on the door, waiting for the deep rumble from the other side.

"Come in."

She slowly pushes one of the doors open, allowing me to step inside. As soon as I'm over the threshold, I find the man in question. He's dressed in a dark pair of slacks and a gray shirt, which has the sleeves rolled up to his elbows, offering me a view of his strong, muscled arms. Veins thread their way down to his fingers, and I find myself squirming. His jaw is dusted with stubble, darkening it slightly. He isn't wearing a tie, and the top two buttons of his shirt are undone.

"Cayleigh." He smiles. I realize then I've been staring for far too long. Lifting my eyes to meet his gray ones, I notice a glimmer of amusement shining in them.

"Hello, Oliver." I smile. With him, I'm shy. It's as if he switches on a button, and suddenly, I'm a nervous teenager.

"Sit." He gestures to the chair opposite his desk. "Did you do as I asked?"

Once I'm situated on the seat, I nod. "Yes, no panties."

"Good girl," he coos in *that* voice. It's the one he used last night in the playroom. When he was with Willow, just those two words give me the need to do anything he wants. "Thank you for sending the contract through," he tells me. "I see you have a list of hard limits you're not willing to try."

"Yes, Oliver."

"So, it's a definite no to me fisting your pretty little pussy?" He chuckles.

My face heats, and I'm certain I'm a bright shade of cherry red at that moment. I open my mouth to respond, but I can't find the words. I've never been a prude, but my inexperience is evident with this man.

"It's a shame. I'm certain I would've made it good for you."

"I-I—"

"Don't. I'm only teasing you," he offers. "Remember,

I'm here for you. To ensure you get the most out of this. I did notice you didn't cross exhibitionism off the list?" He seems shocked at this.

"I find it intriguing."

He watches me silently, then nods. "Stand." I obey. "Walk over to the window. Face the city below us. This may not be ideal because I'd rather you were naked in front of at least ten men while they watch me use you for my pleasure, but this will have to do for the moment."

Oliver doesn't sound like he's joking this time. No. He's deadly serious, and the thought of that happening only makes me wetter. I've never tried it before, but the idea of being taken like that, turning others on, causes a flutter of butterflies in my stomach.

I'm facing the window, wondering what's about to happen next, when I feel his warmth behind me. Since his body is larger than mine, I can feel his thick erection pressing against my ass. It excites me, and we haven't even started yet.

He reaches around me, gently tugging my top out of the waistband of my skirt. Once it's on the floor beside me, he continues, undoing the zipper on the back of my skirt. It pools at my feet, and I'm left in a pair of heels and my bra.

The bra is next to find the floor. And soon, I'm only in four-inch heels —naked and needy. He kicks my one foot out, spreading my legs wide. And I've never been so turned on in my life.

OLIVER

Obedient.

Innocent.

Sensual.

Those are the three words that come to mind when I look at Cayleigh. Even though she's so new to everything, her curiosity is what enamors me to her. It's been a while since a sub has intrigued me.

She doesn't move away from me. Even though there's a shiver that travels through her, it's slight. Her breaths are already short and fast, and I know soon she'll be begging for me to allow her to come.

Trailing my fingertips along her curves, I smile when I notice the goosebumps that appear on her smooth skin. When I reach her nipples, I gently tug and tweak them until they're hard.

"Do you like the fact that people might see you?" I question, allowing my words to whisper along her skin.

"Yes, I do."

"I can smell your cunt from here. You're so wet and needy." My words cause her to shudder, and I wonder if anyone has spoken dirty to her. "It's a shame there aren't any men on the other side of this window with their cocks in hand while you get fucked." My words whisper over her, and the slight shiver in her frame causes my blood to heat with desire and need. I'm almost certain she's never been watched while doing something like this, but the thought of it only makes my cock throb even more.

Another shiver races over her body. My fingers find her pussy. A small trail of hair is neatly trimmed on her mound, leading down to where her clit is hiding.

"Tell me, pet . . . Have you ever felt the lick of a leather belt on your ass?"

"No, Sir."

Stepping back, I release her, eliciting a frustrated groan which rumbles in the depths of her throat. I unbuckle my belt, tugging it from the loops of my slacks. The clank earns me a jolt from Cayleigh. She can't see what I'm doing, but the sounds must have her wanting to run.

"I won't do anything you don't want me to." It's important for her to understand that. "You have your safe words. In any scene, you call them out if you need to. Do you understand?"

"Yes, I understand, Sir."

As much as I know she'll move on to find another Dominant someday; I find myself jealous of whoever he may be. She's exquisite.

"I'm going to give you six swats with my hand to start, then if you want more, I'll try the belt," I inform her. "You'll count each one. Am I understood?"

"Of course, Sir."

Raising my hand, I bring my palm down on her ass. The creamy flesh turns a soft shade of pink. It's hardly there, but I can see it.

"One."

I continue my spanking, watching her knees wobble with each one.

"T-two."

With every word she utters, her voice turns from a soft, shy mumble, to a husky, trembled moan. By the time she reaches four, her ass is a darker red, which makes my cock throbs in my slacks. I'd love to drive into her tight heat, but I've learned patience is well worth it.

"Would you like more?"

"Yes, please, Sir." Her whisper is filled with want and need. She's ready for the next step. I'd want her bound on the bed for this, but she'll have to hold on.

"Place your palms flat on the glass," I instruct her. "I want you to push out your ass. Keep your legs spread wide, and I'll give you four lashings with the belt."

I watch in awe as she obeys me without so much as a grumble. Her body is arched, the slope of her back making my mouth water. I'd love to run my tongue along her spine from the base to the top.

There's a slight sheen to her skin, making her seem ethereal in the light of the afternoon sun on the other side of the window. Cars pass by down below, and even though they can't see her, I wonder if any of the buildings across from us have a voyeur or two.

"You'll count as before."

I don't wait for her to respond. The first lick of leather against the globes of her ass resounds in the office like music to my ears. There are few things I love. One being the cries of a submissive. The other — a kiss of leather against smooth flesh.

"O-one," Cayleigh whimpers, and I gift her another. "T-two." The gentle stutter is the only evidence that she's turned on, that she's experiencing the pleasured pain of my belt.

Red welts appear across both cheeks, and I smile before gifting her another one, the last one before I drop the implement to the ground. It doesn't take long for me to kneel behind her, my hands finding her reddened flesh. Opening her to my gaze, I lean in, darting my tongue to lap at her wet core.

"Oh!"

"Shh, pet." I continue my assault of her cunt, tasting the sweetness of her arousal. Dipping my tongue into her hole, I fuck her with my mouth, gently, slowly massaging the sting from her ass as I devour her.

Her hands are becoming slippery, and her knees

are about to give out when I realize she's about to come on my tongue. I stop before she can, and there's a low growl of frustration that ebbs from her throat. Rising, I step back and pick up her clothes.

"Turn around," I tell her calmly. She turns to regard me, her eyes shimmering with need, but today she'll learn that edging will only make the finale even better. "You'll get dressed, go home, and you will not touch yourself. Tomorrow night, we'll meet at Sins."

"I thought—"

"We will fuck, make no mistake," I inform her, settling in my office chair to watch her get dressed. "But when I slide my dick inside you, it will be when you're ready. And right now, you're not ready."

Once she's dressed, she glances at me for a moment before offering me a shy smile. The innocence is back, hiding the lust-filled gaze from earlier.

"Thank you, Sir," she utters.

"Tomorrow night when you come to Sins, I want you in a long black dress and a pair of four-inch heels. Black lingerie underneath, that will be your choice. Impress me. Am I understood?"

"I understand."

"Good girl," I smile. "Now go enjoy your evening. And do not touch your pretty cunt. I want it ready for me when I fuck it."

She doesn't respond, merely offers a nod and leaves my office and the hard-on I've been sporting since I saw how sensual she looks bent over, open, and shivering as I whipped her. But not only her naked body appeals to me; it's the mind of the masochist hidden under the demure, Irish princess façade.

CHANCE

Even though the apartment is quiet, and I should enjoy it, I don't. All my life, I've always had Peyton around, but now that she's married with children, I'm strangely lonely. I thought to be on my own, I'd revel in it. The moment my sister left for Chicago to see her best friend, Savannah, I spent my nights at the bar, getting drunk, then bringing home women, men, anyone who could fill the emptiness inside me.

Our parents were loving, giving us everything we wanted, but my father had turned a darker path after my mother died. When he lost his life, it was only my sister and me. That's how I became dependent on her. I needed her because, to be honest, I was scared of the pain from losing our parents.

Over time, I realized she needed to live her life too. And when I saw her with Carrick, I knew she'd found her *one.* Me, on the other hand, I was the playboy. I didn't think I wanted love, and now that I'm delving into the world of kink, I'm sure this is something that will ground me. Even after the short scene with Oliver, I know it's a road I'm gladly going to walk down.

Pulling on a shirt, I slowly button it, thinking about Cayleigh, then my mind drifts to Oliver. I'm intrigued by him. The man is so guarded it's as if there's a ten-foot concrete wall wrapped around him. Something must've happened to him, and I can't help wanting to delve into his mind to find out what it is.

The sun is slowly setting on the horizon. The buildings outside my window glint with warmth, and the soft orange glow. Tonight, he promised a scene with Cayleigh, training me as a Dominant. When the message came through to meet him at seven, I responded immediately.

I know he's going to be in control tonight, and seeing him in action, to watch his gray eyes glint, and shimmer only makes my dick jolt. I want to watch him take her, spank her, do things to her while I *learn*. But then again, I want him to do those things to me. The confusion of what I need and what I desire twists in my gut.

I have feelings for both of them—to be submissive to Oliver and to dominate the beautiful Irish girl who's caught my attention. For a long while I thought I was gay, finding certain guys at high school catching my eye, but then I met Sarah just before graduation. She was exquisite. Her long blonde hair and blue eyes turned my blood molten.

We'd gone on a few dates, fooled around, and I enjoyed it. She turned me on, made me want more, and when I slid into her tight heat, I realized I needed to work through so much more.

And that's when I understood there were so many more complex feelings warring inside me. Not just my attraction to guys, but my need for a tight, warm pussy. Sarah and I enjoyed a few nights of fun over the years, but it didn't become more than that. It was pleasurable, and I found out what I enjoyed, but we both knew it wasn't going to be forever.

When I finally confessed to Peyton, she smiled and

offered me a hug, telling me she always knew; she just waited for me to figure it out myself.

That's my sister. Always giving the affection that's needed, and also advice when I don't ask for it. When she suggested I ask Oliver to give me a month and train me, I wasn't sure he'd agree, but now as I get ready to leave to meet him, I'm thankful he did.

Sighing, I grab my keys and head out the door. Tonight is one evening I know I'll never forget. And as the car weaves through the streets, I find the anticipation sizzling through my veins.

Upon entering Seven Sins, I find a few people already at the tables and a couple of men at the bar. Sidling up to the corner seat, I settle and order a drink. From this angle, I can watch everyone. It's always intrigued me seeing how the interactions between the couples are so vastly different.

Some of the women are seated on the laps of the men, others are peering at their hands, with shy smiles on their lips. Some even have a drink they're nursing while the men offer words of explanation or encouragement.

"You're early." Oliver's voice comes from behind

me, causing me to turn. Finding steel gray eyes piercing me, I smile.

"I am. Better to be early than late," I inform him. Something my father had always taught me. Since the moment I could understand, he would drum it into me. *Never be late, son, even for your own funeral. People don't respect tardiness.*

"That's true," Oliver acquiesces, settling in beside me. His hand grasps my glass. Lifting it to his nose, he takes a quick whiff. "Soda," he says in surprise.

"Well, your rules were no drinking when a scene is to be played out."

He nods, a smile turning his lips up at the corners. He looks impressed that I recalled the words on the contract he sent me. I wonder if Cayleigh's read the same, or if that was just personalized for me.

He leans in. Gripping the back of my neck, he pulls me closer. His lips stop inches from mine, his eyes burning a hole right through me, and my dick hardens when his tongue darts out, licking at my lips.

"I'd like to fuck you, outside of the club, not a scene," he tells me in a husky tone. "Perhaps tomorrow, at my place. We'll all have dinner. I want to test Cayleigh's confidence with us."

"I'm sure she'll enjoy it."

He nods. "She'll watch. She'll rub her pretty cunt while I fuck your tight ass." His words send heat skittering through me. "Then I'll watch her suck your cock, and she'll swallow every drop of your release."

I can't stop the moan that rumbles low in my chest, which earns me a sinful smirk from the older man. He's filthy, sexy, and I want every part of him. How I'm going to survive walking away from everything he's offering is still a mystery to me. But perhaps he'll change his mind when the time comes.

I can only hope and pray.

"Hi." The soft, sweet lilt of Cayleigh comes from beside us. Oliver moves away, releasing me and casting his gray eyes on her.

"You look perfect. Both of you are rather fetching this evening," he says, regarding us both with heat in his stormy gaze.

"Thank you," we respond in unison. Cayleigh lets out a shy giggle before Oliver rises, gesturing for us to move to the room where we're about to play out a scene. I'm not sure what's about to happen. All I know is I want every minute to be drawn out. I want to savor it.

OLIVER

As soon as we're in the playroom, I shut the door and lean against the wood. My body is still rigid from the news I received earlier, but they don't need to know what I'm thinking about.

Both my submissives attempt a calm exterior, but I can read them better than they think. There's a slight nervousness to Cayleigh; her hands fidget with everything she touches. It's Chance who seems more at ease with himself.

He settles in the chair, watching me for a moment before he turns his attention to the pretty girl we get to play with tonight. It's been a long time since I had two to train, and it's rather exciting to have them both at my mercy.

"Chance," I call to the man who's enamored me with how easily he can play the role of sub or Dom, depending on what the scene calls for. He rises, standing at attention when I push away from the door and saunter closer.

Reaching for him, I twist my fingers through his unruly golden hair and pull him nearer. His hot breath comes out staggered, and I know he's turned on. He prefers being my submissive, but he loves dominating Cayleigh.

"You're going to undress, lie back on the bed, and I'm going to show you how much pain you can handle. Are you clear on your safe words?" The rasp in my voice is unmistakable. I know he realizes how turned on I am. And I'm sure if I place my hand on his crotch, I'll feel the bulge greeting me.

"Yes, Sir. Red to stop all play," he tells me easily. "I don't need the other two." His confidence oozes from him, emanating like a cologne.

"Fine." Turning to Cayleigh, I offer her a gentle smile before I grab her wrist and tug her along behind me. I have plans to see how beautiful they perform. "Get undressed," I tell her when I open the drawer, pulling out the toys I'll need for tonight.

Clamps.

Cuffs.

Blindfold.

And a cat o' nine tails whip.

Once I step into this room, I'm only a Dominant. A Master at my own game, and that's why both Cayleigh and Chance will obey me.

I move as Chance settles back on the bed. He's naked, and I take a moment to inspect him. The young man is built to perfection. Chiseled, tanned, and toned as if he were trying to get a modeling gig.

His legs are long, and his thighs are thick and muscled. A prominent V defines hips, and his stomach has six visible muscles as he lies there. His cock, which I didn't ignore, is hardening with every passing moment, and I'm confident he's about eight inches.

My gaze trails back to his chest which has well defined pectoral muscles, along with his lean yet toned arms. His neck leads to his face which looks like it could've been carved from marble. His jaw is prominent, his nose sharp, with full pink lips that make my cock throb.

Then I meet his eyes. The same beautiful color of his sister's green—a deep, soulful color that only stirs something I've hidden a long time ago.

Shaking it off, I saunter forward, cuffs in hand and proceed to bind my new submissive to the bed. Once Chance's wrists are tied, I move to his ankles. As soon as he's secure, I smile.

"Cayleigh," I call to the pretty brunette. "I think Chance would like a tease." I gesture toward his cock, which is growing steadily.

A small smile plays on her lips as she regards me. "Yes, Sir." She moves over him, her black lingerie hugging her figure, and I can't help wondering how I got so lucky.

Love may not be in the cards for me, but I'll certainly enjoy them both in the time we have together. I watch in awe as Cayleigh sucks Chance's thick cock into her small mouth. Soft gagging sounds serve to make me harder, my erection fighting against the zipper of my slacks.

Grabbing the whip, I run it through my fingers a few

times before bringing it down on Chance's chest, then his stomach, missing Cayleigh as she works his cock. Groans and grunts echo in the room as those green orbs disappear from sight. Pleasure rockets through him, and I know he's lost in the sensual bliss of Leigh's mouth.

I continue my assault on him until I notice his body turning rigid.

"Stop." My order is clear, and Cayleigh obeys as if she was born into this world. A beautiful pet. The thought brings forth images of her in a cat-tail butt plug and a choker. Shaking the vision away, I focus on the task at hand. I can't get distracted with the needy behavior they both bring out in me.

"Please, Sir, I need to come," Chance pleads. There's nothing like hearing a man beg for his orgasm. Over the years, women and men have come and gone from my dungeon, playroom, and home, but nothing has ever prepared me for this moment.

Right here, as Chance begs me, and Cayleigh stares at me with admiration, I'm a man lost to the need of the scene. To them. I've never felt a connection like this to anyone I've trained before.

"Cayleigh." I turn to the beautiful girl. "I want you naked. Everything off."

She nods and moves quickly. Her bra finds the floor, along with the panties that didn't cover much of her ass or her pretty pussy. She's mostly shaven with a small strip of hair on her creamy mound. I'm tempted to lick her until she's squirting all over my tongue, but I'll wait.

Patience is a virtue. One I no longer possess. What I do hold dear is my control.

"Sit on his face," I command in a low tone, allowing the words to trickle over both of them before Cayleigh's wide stare meets mine. "Now."

She moves quickly, climbing on the bed, and positions herself on Chance's mouth. A soft whimper already falls from her lips as her hips roll, riding his tongue that's slowly lapping at her.

Stepping closer, I can't help but smile as her body trembles. Chance's legs are taut with tension, and his cock is hardening again. I lean in, my hand fisting his erection, causing a groan to rumble in his chest. Stroking him gently, I watch as his body trembles with a need for more.

"Faster, Leigh. I want you to come on his face, drench his tongue in your sweet juices," I command as I grab the whip. Releasing Chance's cock, I raise the whip and bring it down on his thighs while his mouth sucks on the sweet pussy of Cayleigh as she moans sweet whimpers. Her hands pull and tug at his hair, needing more to find her release.

"Cayleigh, stop." My voice sounds around us like an echo. Her body ceases to move. Taking a step toward them, I lean forward, fisting Cayleigh's hair, pulling her closer to me. Our mouths are inches apart. "Rub that pretty pussy for me."

Her hands fall between her thighs, her fingers slipping into her sweetness. My tongue darts out, licking against hers. When I pull away, I glance down at the handsome man who's bound to the bed.

"Lean back, princess," I tell her, before leaning down and licking against his lips. I taste Cayleigh's juices, which are glistening on his mouth. "So, fucking delicious," I growl along his lips.

"I need more," Chance says, breathing along my mouth.

"I know." Smiling, I rise and step back while unbuttoning my shirt. When the material falls to the floor, my slacks follow. "Cayleigh, kiss him. Taste yourself on his lips." She smiles as she obeys my command without hesitation, and I know she'll be a wonderfully obedient submissive.

Watching them kiss is one of the most erotic things I've seen. Her body moves languidly. I know she's close, riding the edge of release. Her pussy hovers over Chance's cock, and I can't help but smile when she shamelessly rubs herself against him.

Her aching body is beautiful as her hips move faster; the kiss swallows her whimpers. Raising the whip once more, I allow it to lick along her back, then his thighs. There's a thick cloud of desire that hangs around us, filling the room like an entity.

I want to lash her, to see her creamy skin redden with welts. I wish for more, but scenes take time to develop. I move to untie Chance's hands, which fall at his sides. He reaches up to grip Cayleigh's hips, holding her steady.

"I'm going to come," he grunts, his eyes flutter closed as pleasure is written on his face. He stills her with tension ripping through his muscles. Veins pop on his forearms, and now I want to see him pleasure me with those tanned fingers.

CHANCE

"I'm going to come," I grunt as pleasure shoots through me. Every nerve in my body is alive and electric. Oliver reaches for my cock, stroking against Cayleigh's wet pussy, causing my spine to tingle as my release empties all over my stomach, overflowing onto her smooth cunt.

I open my eyes to find those big hazel eyes peeking at me under her dark lashes. She's smiling down at me, her body still shaking from the heightened pleasure she's just experienced. I don't know what Oliver plans next, but I can't focus on anything other than his hand on my pulsing dick.

"Cayleigh, your turn on the mattress," Oliver tells her as he wipes her with a soft towel. I'm not sure where he's found it, but I don't care. All I need now is to feel him inside me. My ankles are released from their bindings, and the sweet girl takes my place.

Her legs splay, and I'm met with her beautiful cunt, which is wet and pink.

"You know what to do," Oliver tells me, watching from beside the bed. A glance in his direction tells me he's enjoying the show because he's solid steel. His cock is hard, rigid, and I'm hungry to devour him. To be honest, I want them both.

I turn to Cayleigh. Leaning between her spread thighs, my mouth latches onto her sweet pussy, and my tongue delves into her wetness when I feel the dip of the bed behind me. Oliver's hands are on my ass, massaging me, opening me to his heated stare. It's as if he's burning a hole through me with a mere glance.

"I'm going to fuck you, Chance," he tells me with a low, raspy tone. Cold liquid trickles over my ass, and his fingers circle the tight ring of muscle, causing my cock to jolt, awakening it to half-mast.

He continues his ministrations, and I continue lapping at the sweetest cunt I've ever tasted. My fingers dip into her, feeling her pulse around both digits as I finger her to the edge. Then slowing down and torturing her with nothing more than my tongue flicking her hardened little nub as my fingers taunt her tight opening.

Her hips rise in an attempt to get more friction where she needs it. Pulling away, I glance up at her as I feel Oliver's fingers slipping into me. Two fingers scissor me open slowly, gently. I didn't think this man could be capable of being so tender.

But I need more.

I want him inside me. Pushing back, I groan as he slips a third finger inside while his other hand cups my balls, squeezing just enough to cause me a wince of pleasured pain that sends heat sizzling through me.

"Please, just fuck me," I beg, forgetting my manners because I'm far too gone to even think about calling him Sir. He releases my sac, bringing his palm down harshly on my ass cheek. "Please, Sir," I moan as I ride his fingers, trying to get him to lose control. But this is Oliver Michaelson; he doesn't allow himself to lose control.

His fingers are removed, and I'm about to beg him

again when I feel the head of his cock nudge my opening. Closing my eyes, I suckle Cayleigh's clit into my mouth, grazing it with my teeth as Oliver's cock inches into me. Even though he's moving slow, I feel fuller than I ever have before.

He's thick. Long. And so hard it feels as if he's shoving a steel dildo inside me. Once his hips are against my ass, he stills.

"Fuck," he groans low and almost menacingly as he gives me time to adjust. Or perhaps it's him who needs time to adjust. When he finally moves after long moments, I'm lost in pleasure as I continue devouring Cayleigh, her whimpers and mewls mixed with Oliver's deep growls behind me have me losing myself to the pleasure.

A harsh spank lands on my ass, left, then right, and on and on, until I'm hard again. Oliver grabs my cock, stroking me fast as he fucks me from behind. Our bodies are moving in unison as Cayleigh whimpers she's about to come. Her body is shaking beneath me when I slip three fingers deep inside her and press against that spot at the front of her mound, causing her to squirt all over my mouth, tongue, and hand.

Her flavor is sweet. There's a slight musk to it, but it's beautiful, sexy, and her thighs tremble on either side of my head. Oliver's moving so fast I can't think straight.

"I'm close." My voice is ragged and broken as he causes my body to lock along with his. His cock thickens inside me; his hand tightens around my cock, causing me to spurt white-hot release all over the mattress.

Oliver's heat fills me, and I'm sure there's no longer a reason for me to walk away. I want this man. No matter what he tells me, I know he wants me too.

"What happened after?" Peyton's voice is high-pitched over the line as I inform her about my night with Oliver. I've kept out the details, but I needed advice from my sister about how I tamper down my feelings for the man who claims he can't love.

"Well, we cleaned up, and he sat with us to see how we felt. I guess his idea of aftercare." Shrugging, I sip the coffee that's still too hot while I wait for my sister to respond.

"Oliver is broken," she confesses. "He may come across as being in control, but there's something about him that's always made me feel as if he needs someone to break down those walls."

"Maybe someone broke his heart, and he doesn't want to go through that again," I offer. "I mean, I understand that."

"But you're feeling something more for him. Aren't you?" Her question stills me for a moment before I nod to myself. I am. I can't deny it. At first, I figured it was just because he was unattainable, and I wanted one night with him. But something changed. It has become so much more.

"Maybe." I try to seem nonchalant, but my sister is perceptive, and she knows me far too well.

"Come on, Chance," Peyton sighs. "I've known you all your life. You can't hide anything from me." I can't help but grin at my sister. She's always been there for me.

"Fine, yes, I'm allowing my feelings to get in the way of this."

"Be careful," she warns in a loving tone, and I know

she's not trying to upset me, but my chest tightens when I realize I could want more from Oliver, and it may be something he can't offer me. "I know you're all grown up now, but you're still my brother, and I worry about you."

"You have no reason to worry. I can take care of myself."

She sighs, and I can't help but smile because my sister has always acted like she's the mom between the two of us; even though we're pretty much the same age.

"Look, you have the kids to worry about," I point out with a chuckle. And just then, as if on cue, one of the girl's screeches over the line.

"Fuck," Peyton hisses into the speaker, causing me to laugh out loud. "I have to go. If you need anything—"

"Go look after the girls. I'll see you soon." I hang up before she has time to admonish me for dismissing her. Setting my phone on the counter, I gulp down the now cold coffee. I know she's right. But I feel as if I can get through to him. Perhaps I can make him see we could work.

The shrill beep of a message coming through makes

me jump. When I pick up my phone, I find Cayleigh's name on the screen. Opening the app, I read through her words and smile. She's a sweetheart.

I type out my response before heading to the bedroom to get ready to meet with her. She's asked to meet for coffee, which makes me curious as to what she wants to talk about. I wonder then if she's asked Oliver as well, or if this will just be us.

OLIVER

The office is silent when I enter after my meeting downtown. I have a man to find, and I need to ask Callan if he's able to assist. Carrick's brother has offered me his services if needed, and he's good at what he does. There's no mercy on his part, and that's what I admire. In this business, offering compassion to these assholes is not what I do.

I pull my cell phone from my pocket and press dial on his number. Three rings and his voice comes from the other end of the line. "Oliver," he says in his thick Irish accent.

"Callan, I have a client who needs our help. Are you up for a job?" I question. Settling in my office chair, I glance out the window finding the sun still high in the sky. Summer is one of my favorite seasons, mainly because I get to see beautiful women dressed in next to nothing.

My office door glides open, and Teresa strolls inside with a small smile on her face. She's new. I hired her a week ago, but she's learning what I enjoy. Her slight frame is draped in a yellow summer dress, and by the peaks at the bodice, she's obeyed my order and is not wearing a bra.

Her tits are small but perky, and my cock jolts at the sight. Crooking my fingers, I call her closer and watch as she slowly nears my desk. I point at the chair, wordlessly ordering her to sit, which she does.

"I'm up for anything. You know that." Callan's voice comes through the receiver, and I can't help smiling because I knew he'd take on any job I offer.

"Great. I'll email you the details. And Callan . . . No mercy on this one. I want all the dirt." My voice is low as my sweet little Teresa blushes at my staring.

"Will do. Thanks, Oliver." He hangs up before I can respond.

Setting my phone on the desk, I rise, shrugging off

my jacket. "How are you today, pet?" I question as I hang the suit jacket on the back of my chair.

"I'm fine," she whispers, causing me to turn my gaze on her again. Her hands are twisting around each other in her lap, and I wonder if she's not wearing any panties either.

"You've been a good girl, I see." I gesture with my chin toward her tits.

Her cheeks darken with a rosy shade, which makes me smile. "I did. Also," she murmurs as she rises, pulling the hem of her dress along up her thighs. When she reaches her hips, I notice her sweet little cunt is bare.

"Well." I smile. Stepping closer to her, I allow my hungry gaze to trail along those creamy thighs, landing on the slit she's shaven, leaving a small patch of dark hair just above where her clit is probably pulsing at the fact that she's flashing me. "That's a rather lovely view," I tell her, noticing movement at my office door.

I know who it is without looking at her. I focus on this stunning woman who's making my cock hard. "Thank you, Sir." She blushes again. Lowering her dress, she sits back down on the chair, and I lift my gaze to the doorway.

"Are you going to stand there watching me, or would you like to come inside and join the fun?" I question Cayleigh. She's open to trying new things like last night with Chance, but this may be just out of her area of limits.

"Sure." She nods with a smile as she shuts the door behind her. When she nears me, I reach for her, slipping my fingers through her hair, tugging her chocolate locks toward me. Her lips part on a gasp as I lean in, allowing my lips to whisper along hers.

"You've just had a coffee," I tell her, licking along the plump, pink flesh of her mouth. "I like that," I tell her. Pushing my tongue into her mouth, I allow her to suck on it until my cock is jolting with need. I want to feed her my dick.

"Sir." Teresa's soft voice alerts me she's still in the office. "Shall I go?"

"No." Pulling Cayleigh to my desk, I push her face down along the smooth surface and whip her skirt over her ass. She's wearing a tiny pair of white lace panties, which I grip in my fist and rip from her body. "Eat her pussy."

"What?"

"You heard me," I tell the shy girl. "Unless you need me to cane your pretty little ass."

She rushes as she kneels behind Cayleigh whose legs are spread enough to get to her pretty cunt. I watch as Teresa's tongue snakes out and licks along Leigh's smooth little pussy, which makes me want to stroke my cock, but I hold back, as I watch the scene unfold before me.

"Oh god," Cayleigh whimpers when the girl leans in farther, her hands holding onto Cayleigh's thighs as she goes to town, eating pussy like it's part of her job. Well . . . It sort of is. I watch as my submissive is reaching her peak when I grip the brown hair of Teresa and tug her backward.

"Enough."

"Please, Sir," Cayleigh begs, but I ignore her.

"Thank you, Teresa, I'll see you tomorrow." Dismissing the pretty girl, I shove her toward the door before turning my attention to Cayleigh. "Stand." She obeys me, turning to face me. "I want you to tell me what you desire. Delve into that mind and give me your darkest fantasy."

I round the desk and settle in my chair once more. I know what Leigh wants, but I need her to voice it. I need the words before I ever enact her need.

She watches me for a moment before sitting in the chair opposite my desk. I don't look at her; instead, I send Callan the email I promised. The sooner he can get on that job, the better. I'd like to have this asshole behind bars before tomorrow night comes.

I promised his wife he'll be locked away for a very long time, and knowing Callan, he'll ensure I have the evidence I need to make it happen.

"I have many fantasies," Cayleigh finally admits.

Nodding, I respond, "I know." I sit back and cast my gaze on her. "But there's one, in particular, I want you to tell me about." She flushes red, and I realize she's probably never told anyone about it.

I've found over the years it's not an uncommon fantasy among women. Yes, there are some who would be triggered by it, but there are those who need it. They crave it — a man taking advantage.

"Does your pussy get wet when you think about it?"

She lowers her gaze, which makes my palm twitch to spank her. I want her eyes on me, but I don't force the issue. She needs to come to terms with her needs. This is why I do what I do. Women and men are so scared to be honest about their desires. I'm here to coax it out, to show them it's not shameful. There's something beautiful about dipping into the darkness and enjoying something others don't.

"When you spread your legs at night and rub your cunt, do you come thinking about it?" My voice is raspy when I question her again, causing her to snap her beautiful eyes to mine.

"I do." She nods slowly, ashamed of what her needs are, and it frustrates me. I want to bend her over and whip her ass with my belt to make her see there's nothing to feel guilty about.

"Then tell me, Cayleigh. We're both adults here. I can give that to you. Fulfill your fantasy in a safe environment." Steepling my fingers, I rest my elbows on the desk, pinning her with a curious gaze as I wait for her.

"I want . . . God, this is stupid." She sighs. "I want a CNC scene." Her words fall from her mouth in a rush, and her cheeks turn bright red.

"Consensual non-consent," I say the words outright so she can agree. I've done this a few times. Allowed the submissives to find the pleasure they need within this type of scene, and normally I wouldn't do it with a day-old submissive, but I've known Cayleigh since she arrived from London. "And that's what you want to experience?"

"Yes, I do." She straightens her back. Her gaze meets mine as she lifts her chin in confidence. Surprising me as I didn't think she'd have when admitting her desires. Even though she's still blushing, she's smiling. "I want that scene, Oliver. But it must only be us."

"Fine." I nod. "Just us. Tonight, you'll be at home. You'll wear what you normally wear to bed." Sitting back, I cross my ankle over the opposite knee while I take her in. "And you'll not know when I will arrive."

"Yes, Sir."

"Go." She rises with a small grin and leaves me to think about how I'm going to do this. I should do it at the club, in one of the back rooms, but that's not realistic at all. No, tonight I'll show Cayleigh how much pleasure can be found in pain.

Shrugging on my jacket, I take one last look in the mirror. Seeing the man I've become, I would never have expected to be wearing a suit and tie, going to work every day where I own two lucrative companies and have men and women at my beck and call.

My younger years were filled with so much darkness that there are times I look at my life now and realize I worked so hard to get where I am today. As a teenager, I was nothing more than a lazy youngster with nothing ahead of me, nothing to look forward to.

My father and I were always at odds. He would shout and scream, telling me I would regret my laziness. And one day it finally hit me, the idea of never getting out of the small town I lived in. I felt claustrophobic, and I knew I had to do something.

Over time, I realized my father was afraid of me never making a name for myself. One of the seven deadly sins had me in its feral grip, holding on so tight I wasn't sure it would ever let me go.

Sloth.

I lazed around the house every weekend. I didn't go out and enjoy life, but I had an excuse. I was bullied. I didn't want to face people, but the more my father forced me from the house, the more I realized if I could get out of the one-horse town, I'd be okay.

Nobody knew me when I got to college. Nobody taunted me because I wanted to spend the night with a guy instead of a busty blonde or brunette. But it was only when I met Paolo did things change.

The pleasure that coursed through my veins having a beautiful, naked woman and a handsome, naked man bending to my will. It's how my Dominant side rose and awoke.

It was all I needed to find out who I was finally. And I didn't let go. I gripped it with both hands, holding tight to the need living inside me.

Now, as I make my way down to the garage, I feel pride settling in my chest. This is all my hard work paying off. It may have taken years to come, but when it arrived, I knew I would never let success go. I would never be that youngster lying on the sofa, not wanting to work toward goals.

Tonight, my goal is to devour a beautiful body with elicit moans and sweet pleasure. With a smirk on my face, I slip into the driver's seat and hope my sweet Cayleigh is ready for an evening of debauchery.

CAYLEIGH

I've never been so fucking nervous in all my life. All day, my mind has been awash with what Oliver offered. I'm finally going to experience a scene which I've wanted for so long, and I can't remember a time when I haven't fantasized about it.

Only one other man has given me something I needed so much, and he was murdered in cold blood. Granted, we didn't explore a dark scene like this. We only enjoyed our rough fucks on occasion, but I always craved more, and even then, he couldn't deliver. Maybe it's because he loved me too much.

The night is dark, with only a sliver of the moon peeking through the curtains. Sipping my wine, I close my eyes in an attempt to calm my nerves. I should put some music on to fill the silence, but I can't bring myself to stand up. My knees are wobbly, and my legs are shaky.

Staring into the depths of the wine, I swirl the crimson fluid against the edges. I focus on the shimmering lights reflecting in the glass. Red wine is my vice. It always has been. When I was younger, out partying, I'd drink copious amounts of the alcohol. It got to a point where I would be numb from the effect of drinks I'd consumed.

I was sixteen the first time I drank wine. Or beer for that matter. Living with an Irish mobster for a father and having two older brothers who didn't want you around because you were the annoying little sister caused me to hang out with the wrong crowd.

The girls who hung around our house only wanted to see my father or fuck my brothers. Hell, I think some of them fucked my father too. I can't help shuddering at that. I decided I'd be the grown up and get to know them, make friends with them so I could also be part of their clique. And that's when I met *him,* the man who stole my heart and gave me a ring.

Of course, my father wanted to kill Sean since I was his baby girl. What my father soon realized was that

I'd grown up way too fast. Most of my childhood was learning about guns, about who's on the wrong side of the fence and who's on the right.

I didn't go to the clubs or cinemas. I spent my time watching men bow down to Pa rather than see what other girls my age did. I don't regret my life, not at all, but now that I'm here and I have the freedom to do as I wish without the whole mob watching over me, I plan to explore who I am as a woman.

I want to live out my fantasies, my dreams, and that brings me back to now. I've made a decision that I need to talk to Oliver and Chance about. At first, I thought I'd be one-third of this relationship. But I've made up my mind. I'd like to have a relationship where it will only be my Dominant and me. Also, I can see there's emotion between them, and as much as I try, I don't feel the same for either of them.

As much as I care for Oliver and Chance, I know my life isn't here. And I want to find out who I am before delving into a long-term relationship. Oliver's training will prepare me, and I know I'll be ready for when the time comes.

The other conversation I'm not looking forward to having is telling Carrick and Callan I want to leave. I love my brothers, but they're the epitome of demanding assholes. I know they love me, and they're looking out for me, but it's time for me to walk on my own. I've thought long and hard, and I'm going to call Eva and see if I can live with her and Nate in Los Angeles. It's time for me to spread my wings once more.

Nathan is one of Carrick's best friends, and he and his wife Eva have a family now. Nate runs Seven Sins LA. I'll be safe and have the support of what I would call extended family. If my brother trusts them, I know they're good people.

Rising from the chair, I head into the kitchen to refill my glass when my body is flung away from the countertop, the glass shattering to the floor, and I'm pressed against the cool wall beside the fridge.

"If you scream, I'll make this even worse for you," Oliver's rough timbre whispers in my ear, low and menacing. My knees go weak, and my clit thrums. His one hand grips my wrist behind my back, his other fisting my long brown hair as he tugs me backward. "Do you understand me, pet?"

"Y-yes," I stammer, realizing my heart is hammering wildly, but even though there's a hint of fear, I'm more turned on than I've ever been before. Ever.

He wordlessly drags me toward the hallway, straight down toward my bedroom. He releases me only for a second before gripping both my wrists and slamming my back against my bedroom door. His eyes, normally a steel gray, turn dark, menacing as if a raging thunderstorm is about to hit.

The corner of his mouth tilts into a grin — devious and sadistic. His free hand reaches for my shorts, tugging them down my legs.

"Please, Oliver, we don't have—"

"Did I fucking ask you to speak?" he hisses, gripping my throat, tightening his hold on me. My pussy is wet, as I'm needy for this man.

"N-no, Sir," I whisper. Tears form in my eyes, pricking against the lashes, and I blink, allowing them to fall. His smile is pure venom. He's lost in this scene, and I'm trembling with want.

He shoves me down to my knees, my head banging

against the wall, which has stars momentarily flashing behind my lids as he holds me steady. Without much effort, his cock is out, jutting from the open zipper.

"Open," he grunts, pushing the tip against my lips. I can't *not* obey him, and the tears streaming down my face only seem to make him harder as I watch the shaft jolt when he scrutinizes me. My lips part, and his cock slams in deep. My throat constricts around it, making gagging sounds as he fucks my face with wild abandonment.

My hands push against his thighs, attempting to move him backward, but his stance is solid, and his body moves against mine like it was made to piston in and out of me. There's desire emanating around the room — thick and muggy.

My stomach lurches when he pushes deeper. I can feel the bulge in my throat and the burn rising up in my gullet, he pulls back. Spit drips from the thick, angry shaft in strings, as I've seen in porn.

"Such a pretty girl when you cry," he tells me, slamming down my throat one more time for good measure. He grips his cock, slapping it against my cheek. "This is what you wanted." The words make my heart soar.

I'm wrenched from the floor, dragged across the room, and pushed onto the bed. In an attempt to get away, I'm pulled back by my ankles. A harsh, burning swat on my ass causes me to cry out as the sting tingles through me.

He tugs my shorts down my thighs, finding my thong and chuckling. He doesn't wait, merely tears it from my body, the material ripping loudly in the room. The only sounds that echo in my ears are my whimpers and his grunts.

My bedside lamp flies from the nightstand, crashing onto the floor. My erratic heartbeat thuds wildly in my chest; my lungs protest as I play the role. The bedding torn from the perfectly made bed makes it look like there's been a war inside my room.

His body is on me, heavy and commanding. His cock prods against the crack of my ass. I'm clawing at the bed, my nails digging into the sheets, but it's no use. I'm five foot nothing, and he's over six feet. I have no chance.

His hands are in my hair once more, pulling my

head backward, his lips at my cheek. "So fucking good," he growls the moment he slams into my pussy, which is drenched. I cry out as the thickness of his cock spreads me painfully, but pleasure zings along my spine. Every nerve ending in my body is alight with an electric current that sends me into orbit.

"Please, Oliver," I whimper once more, knowing my safe words but not using them. And that's when he finally takes me.

OLIVER

I pull out of her, waiting for her to whimper in frustration. "Is this what you wanted?" My voice is thick, husky with desire. I'm a sadist; this shit is what I live for. Her body is trembling beneath me, and I know she can feel my cock pressing into her back. Knowing she's scared is part of what kicks my adrenaline into high gear.

"Please," she croaks, her voice turning hoarse with the scream I wrenched from her moments ago. I've always found "cat and mouse" to be a fun game, but when you add in the element of desire that thrums through her veins and burns in her gaze, it makes it so much more elicit.

Pulling her off the bed, I smile down at her slim

frame and press her against the plush carpet. Watching her claw against practically nothing makes me chuckle. I'm lost in the scene. I'm obliterating my need and hers. My hands are on her again, spanking her harder and harder. My hand is burning, her ass turning a bright shade of red.

"Do you want me to fuck you right here on the floor?" I lean in and hiss in her ear. "Tell me, Cayleigh, do you need my cock breaking your tight pussy?" My words whisper over her neck as I latch onto her soft flesh, sucking it hard into my mouth until she's squealing.

"Sir, please, Oliver, no," she whimpers and moans, but her body betrays every utterance because she lifts her hips, pushing her ass against my crotch, and I know she's taunting me as much as I am her. My hand around her throat is tight, squeezing the air from her lungs when she finally bucks me off and rolls onto her back.

It doesn't take me long to grab her ankle as she's trying to escape and drag her back to the floor. The carpet underfoot is soft enough that when she topples, there's only a soft whooshing sound. She's once again under me, but this time I'm nestled between her straining thighs.

Her cheeks are bright red, her neck a rosy hue, and her lips plump and parted as her breaths come short and quick. She's so turned on she can hardly speak. Her mascara has run down her face leaving pretty, beautiful streaks. She's incredible.

I press two fingers onto her tongue. "Suck," I order, and she does. Her lips clamp down around both digits, and my mind is awash with images of her choking on my cock again. I want her to gag once more. I want to hear those pretty sounds she makes. Tugging my hand from her, I reach between her legs and pump two fingers into her. She's nowhere near wet — she's fucking drenched.

"Please, Sir," she mewls, lifting her hips toward me. And I know she needs it. Her orgasm is close. I feel her walls pulsing around my fingers, and I continue taunting her. The moment I feel her tighten, I stop all movement, which makes her body shudder and convulse.

A smirk on my lips makes her tear up. She knows I'm torturing her. We both needed this. Ached for it. The air is heavy with lust, so fierce it threatens to burn the fucking building down, but all I can think of is bending her to my will.

"Are you ready to come on my cock?" I don't wait for her to answer. My hand is already gripping my shaft, and I'm plunging into her. The force with which I drive my hips into hers knocks all breath from her lungs.

I pull out, thrusting my cock into her again and again. We're breathing heavy as I grip her wrists, pinning them onto the carpet, holding her down. I don't relent. Her orgasm slams into her, causing her to scream my name, but she doesn't call her safe word.

There's no way I can stop the feeling as it trickles up my spine. Each whimper and moan is fuel to the fire burning and raging itself through my veins. My blood burns as it scorches my need for Cayleigh.

The sound of sex is heavy in the air, and we're merely animals, needing our release. Her juices drench me, but I don't stop fucking her into the floor when she once more tries to wiggle her way from underneath me. My cock throbs, spearing into her. I don't see reason anymore because the only thing that matters is her. Completely and utterly letting me own her.

I throb inside her tight heat, expanding, thickening to the point of spreading her tight hole to take me. I want this. She needs it, and as she latches her mouth onto my shoulder, her teeth sink into my skin, drawing blood as I empty my seed inside her.

My chest heaves against her tits. Our bodies are sweaty, and I'm trembling as much as she is. I know that was something I'll never experience again. The first time with a new submissive in a specific scene or role play is always something extraordinary for me.

"Oliver," she whispers in my ear, bringing me back down to earth, to reality, where I've got her pinned down like a rag doll. She looks broken — her hair is a mess, and those pretty eyes are shimmering with tears. Plump lips are swollen from our kiss and parted in an O. Her cheeks are stained with black streaks of her emotion, when I face-fucked her for my pleasure.

Utterly fucking beautiful.

"Cayleigh." My voice is still thick and raspy. "Are you okay?" Lifting my head, I meet her teary gaze. I've never seen a more stunning woman than her right now. There's something primal about her, and all I can think about is leaning in to lap at the salty liquid shining on her face. Tears drip down the sides toward her ear, and I take them in my mouth, licking her pain, her desire, her fear.

"I've never been better." Her smile lights up her face, and I know I've offered her something she clearly needed. In all my years of being a Dominant, I'd never allowed myself to lose complete control. I'd never even fathomed wanting it like that. Yes, I love the pain, doling out on supple flesh, but I can't explain how this has completely cracked me open and laid me bare. It takes me back to a memory that shudders through me. My chest aches in agony as I recall it with clarity.

There's blood everywhere. I can't breathe. Two sets of eyes burn holes through me. They're smiling, wicked, evil, and vile. I can't move. The pain is too much. My lungs attempt to pull in air, but as I shift, I realize there's a keening cry coming from somewhere.

Guilt weighs heavily on me.

There's a pain so acute shooting through every nerve in my body. I open my mouth, but nothing comes out. I see it as if I'm having an out-of-body experience. They're satisfied with what they've done. What they've made me do. My body is cold, rigid, and I pray for death to steal me.

"Good lad." The deep rumble comes from beside me. A slap on the back in camaraderie and bile rises in my throat, burning like acid. Racing for the trash can, I lose the contents of my stomach. There's not much, but the bitter taste has more to do with what I've just done than the puke that tumbles over my lips.

Tears streak down my face when I realize how broken I truly am. They made me this way — broken inside and out.

"Get him up. We need to clean this mess before your wife gets home." The chuckle of a man I trusted all my life is clear, sharp as a blade slicing through me. I don't know how I'll survive this.

Turning my gaze on those blue eyes that stare at me emotionlessly, I utter the only words I can offer. "I'm sorry."

"I'm sorry." Shoving away from her, I stumble backward, unsure of what else to say. The awareness that suddenly hits me is fierce, threatening to choke me. "I . . ." Rising to my feet, I offer her my hand, which she accepts with a shy smile. "That was . . . I shouldn't have lost control like that."

"I know I was safe with you." Her tiny hand lands on my heaving chest as I try to pull in air. My lungs feel as if they're filled with concrete, and it only serves to make me more anxious. I pride myself on my control, on how well I handle this life, but Cayleigh does something to me. She breaks down the Dominant hold I have and wiggles her way into my darkness.

"Cayleigh, we will never do that again."

"Are you trying to tell me if I called out my safe word, you wouldn't have stopped?" she bites out in frustration, and I know I've just messed with our evening. I promised her a night where she'd be able to let go, to live out what she desires, and now I've fucked it up.

"I need to go home. Get dressed." Racing from the room, I make my way into the second bedroom. Needing silence, I shut the door behind me, allowing myself a moment to breathe. The memory of what I was forced to do because sick individuals wanted entertainment haunts me. The girl was broken, but so was I. Two men who were meant to be guardians, adults, took what wasn't theirs to take from her and me.

My shirt is torn, my hair is a mess, and there's a bite mark on the curve of my neck which can thankfully be hidden by the collar of my jacket or shirt.

The click of the door sounds behind me, and then I hear the soft footfalls of Cayleigh, alerting me of her presence in the small room. How I wish I were home right now in my private space.

"What are you doing?"

"I wanted to see if you were okay," she tells me confidently.

Pivoting, I meet her wide eyes which are so pretty, they're sparkling like gemstones. "There will never be a day you top me from the bottom. I am the one who takes care of you," I tell her. I notice her flinch at my harsh words, at me pushing her affection away.

"This life," she waves her hand around us. "It's what I need. I asked for that, and you gave it. I'm not some brainless idiot who cannot make choices for myself. I'm not trying to top you. I'm not even trying to push you away, but there's something inside here," she says, placing two fingertips on my forehead, "that's scaring you. What is it?"

Stalking toward her, I grip her arms, shoving her backward until her body is slammed between mine and the wall behind her. She doesn't flinch; she doesn't even mewl.

"I don't deal well with affection."

"And I don't deal well with assholes," she bites out, earning her a chuckle. Her lips purse in a tight line, making me hungry to feast on them.

"If you ever speak to me like that again, I will tan your ass," I warn her. "Now, I trust you're ready for me to leave?"

"Do you want to leave? Or are you pushing me away?" Her question stills me for a moment, and I realize she's right. Yes, I should've given her aftercare. I'm failing at the only thing that's ever given me pleasure after a scene — something I'd always prided myself in. I'm becoming lazy in my dominance, which is not a good thing. Without a word, I scoop her into my arms, carrying her bridal-style into her bathroom.

Once in the small room, I set her down and start undressing her. She allows me to work without her sassy mouth, and I'm thankful. I'm so focused on what I'm doing that I don't realize by the time she's naked her cheeks are glistening with tears.

"I've failed you." My words are a harsh whisper, but she shakes her head in response.

"It's been a long time since someone has taken such care with me." She steps closer to me; her tiny hands holding my shoulders, then she trails them down to slowly unbutton my shirt and push it over my shoulders until it falls to the floor.

I watch in awe as she takes care of me the same way I did her. Once we're both naked, I realize we're both baring more than just our bodies at this moment. And I've never been so fucking scared of a woman in my life.

OLIVER

Last night, I took Cayleigh. And after our scene, we both cared for each other in a way I'd never done with any of my other subs. I allowed her in, into the darkest depths of my mind. And she, in turn, allowed me into her body once more before I left. She fell asleep on her bed, and I covered her with a blanket and walked out into the night.

I couldn't stay. There wasn't anything that would've kept me there last night. I drove for hours. Even when the sun came up, I continued to put my foot on the gas pedal and drove. I left the city and came back again. If someone asked where I was, I couldn't tell them, but I needed to think.

With all my training, every year that passed, I never once played out a scene that brought me back to that time of my life. I'd locked it away in a dark corner of my mind and promised myself never to live through it again. But last night, something crashed to the ground along with Cayleigh's body and mine, and I lost it. The hidden memory slammed into me with a ferocious clarity.

I couldn't tell her what happened. There was no way I could admit what I'd been through, so instead of being honest, I brushed it away like it was nothing. I didn't allow myself to wallow in the images that flashed through my mind.

Her sweet-scented perfume invaded my nostrils and brought me back to the present. My heartbeat that seemed to want to break through my rib cage calmed to normal. I wasn't in *that* house. I was beside her. Holding on to one of the most beautiful people I've ever met. I forced myself to hold her, to stroke her hair after brushing it. I needed the gentle after the roughness. And she allowed me to work through the ghosts haunting me.

When I pull into the driveway, I stare at my home for a long while before exiting the car and making my way inside. The house I bought when I finally made it in the city is modern, with not a lot of furniture or even photos of the family I never had.

Taking in the space now, I realize how empty my life is. I know Cayleigh is leaving. There's a sadness to her, and I know she needs to go. She needs to find herself, which brings me back to my other student.

Since Chance first walked into the club, I had a feeling he was going to be a challenge. And after being with him, I know for sure I want more. For years, I've been content with training and walking away. But for some reason, Chance has intrigued me. There's something about him, his smile, those piercing eyes that seem to look right through me. I crave to see him submit to me.

Pulling my cell phone from my pocket, I hit dial on his number. It's already nine in the morning, so he should be up.

"Oliver?" His voice comes from the other end of the line, the tone thick with sleep, and I realize I've woken him.

"I thought you'd be up by now. I'm sorry for waking you," I tell him as I head into my kitchen to make coffee.

"No, it's okay," he assures me, and I can hear the smile in his voice.

Setting the mug under the tap, I lean against the counter. "I'd like a scene with you. Privately. Just you and me."

"Okay."

"How about tonight?" I offer, holding my breath like a damn teenager. I like Chance; there's something real about him. He's not one of those clingy assholes who tend to annoy me. He's mature, his own person, and I know if we did continue on after our contract is up, I'd enjoy him immensely.

"Sure, what time?"

Coffee drips into the mug. Once it's ready, I pick it up and take a small sip. The caffeine immediately hits my senses. "How about we meet around seven?" I tell him. "We'll have dinner, and I can show you my playroom."

"And Cayleigh?"

"She and I had a scene last night." I swallow past the lump of emotion in my tone, remembering how beautifully erotic it was, but also, how much I scared myself. I'd lost all sense of control.

"Okay, I'll be there." His smile is evident in his voice, and I picture his eyes lighting up with excitement. He's a beautiful boy, a handsome young man, and I look forward to seeing just how he'll take to the scene I have in mind.

"Wear something formal."

He's silent for a while, and I wonder if he's dropped the call, but then he responds in a lower tone. "I can do that for you." His words cause my cock to harden, and I can't help but smile.

"Good. See you tonight."

Hanging up, I make my way into the bedroom and set the mug on the nightstand. I make quick work of undressing and taking in the bruise on my neck in the mirror. Cayleigh is a naughty minx for that.

Walking into my bathroom, I turn on the shower to ready myself for the day ahead.

The day has been busy. Callan's almost got all the information I need to proceed with taking down a high-profile politician. Stalking into the house, I shut the door behind me and head up to my bedroom. My tie is loose, and I tug it free, unbutton my shirt, and pull it from the waistband of my trousers.

Toeing off my shoes, I step into the bathroom and open the cold water tap to splash some on my face. The stress of the day has gotten to me, but if I had to be honest with myself, it's more about the Irish princess than anything else.

Grabbing a towel, I dab my face and make my way down to the living room, leaving my shirt unbuttoned. In the corner, I perch against the bar, pouring a hefty shot of Scotch before downing it in one long gulp. My throat burns with fire as it trickles its way down into my chest.

I have a few moments before Chance arrives, and I have no idea if I even want to play this scene out. After last night, all I want is to feel someone, to take them in my own way. The fantasies I offer, the scenes I gift my submissives are nothing short of what they choose. I delve into their minds, find what it is they most crave, and give it to them in a safe environment.

With every submissive, I allow myself to get lost in my need. Watching them come apart at my touch, or my words, it satisfies me more than I could've imagined.

They're all different, unique in their wants and needs, but ultimately, they're searching for, attempting to quench the thirst that lies dormant within them. And after the first scene, that's when they come alive.

Most people are too afraid to admit what they long for. I've met submissives who are afraid to be honest with themselves at the pleasure they derive from kneeling, giving up control, or even being handled roughly.

Society has made sure we're all afraid of our basic wants. Sexual fantasies are played out behind closed doors because we're scared of being judged. It's sad to see it happen, but that's why I find Seven Sins such an incredible space. It allows those who need the openness to explore without society telling them it's wrong.

Closing my eyes, I focus on clearing my mind of the thoughts that seem to invade it. Since yesterday, and till now, I've been plagued by what happened. Nobody knows. I haven't ever found anyone I wanted to share that part of myself with.

Perhaps it's the fear of being judged, or maybe it's the agonizing pain of reliving it to someone. To voice the words that always get stuck in my throat, threatening to choke me.

Even my father doesn't know. All he thinks is my younger years were spent as a lazy asshole hiding in his room. But what he doesn't know is, his son lost everything because of how nature made him.

I had no choice who I cared for. I didn't want to be different from the rest of my classmates, but I was. At that time, in a small town in America, being bisexual was a sin. The pastor would talk about it on a Sunday. He would admonish those emotions that flared when we came of age, and every child in that parish knew it was the work of Satan.

Chuckling, I pour another steep shot and swallow it down before I settle in the armchair, watching the lights of the city twinkle on from my living room window. I wonder what I should do about my father. I walked out and vowed I'd never go back, but with him getting older, frailer than ever before, I know the time will soon come when I need to return to that hell and bury him.

Even the thought of seeing his body lowered into a grave doesn't make me sad. Losing one's parents should be heartbreaking, but I no longer feel that for him. Once he's gone, I'll say goodbye to my past and move on. At least, that's what I tell myself.

I'm about to grab another drink when the buzzer alerts me Chance has arrived.

Time to play and forget this shit.

CHANCE

When the door opens, I'm met with a force of fucking nature.

Oliver Michaelson is not an ordinary man. He's a hurricane that rips through every part of you and leaves a wake of destruction in his path. The shirt he's wearing is unbuttoned with the smooth, tanned skin peeking at me, and there's a smattering of hair on his chest. Allowing my gaze to trail down to his stomach, I take note of his perfect body. You can tell he takes care of himself.

"Chance." He breathes my name in a low rumble that reminds me of why I'm here. When he invited me to dinner this evening, I vowed to finally admit what I'm feeling for him, that I'd like more than just a training contract from him. I want to be his, to fully submit to him.

"Oliver, it's good to see you." I smile, offering him a slight nod.

"Come in." He steps back, allowing me into his space. The personal space I'd never seen, but as soon as I enter, I know it's his home. Even though there are modern lines, there's a dim yellow light that gives the illusion of candlelight. It's calming.

He shuts the door behind me, guiding me into the living room furnished in cream-colored sofas, black shag carpet, and a large fireplace, which almost seems out of place with the exposed brick.

There's a bar in the far-left corner and a floor-to-ceiling window overlooking the city. We're perched higher than most of the buildings in the main section of town, and I'm awed at just how beautiful it is.

"Drink?" Oliver offers from behind me, causing me to pivot and find his steely gaze on me. He's holding a bottle of Scotch, and even though I can't see the label, I know it's expensive. A man like Oliver wouldn't be drinking some random shit. It would be top shelf.

"Yes, please."

He pours my drink and settles in the armchair beside me. There's a silence between us, hanging in the air, but it's not uncomfortable. Oliver glances at me, taking me in, and his roving eyes make me self-conscious.

"Thank you for coming tonight," he finally says, his hand trailing the suede of the armchair, his fingertips brushing the material ever so lightly, and I find myself mesmerized by the beautiful intricate patterns he's making. His hands are strong but gentle, and I want them on me. I want to feel his fingers stroking me.

"I wanted to spend time with you."

"Is that so?" The corner of his mouth quirks. The corner of his eyes crease as he regards me with something akin to affection. "Sorry, I don't normally do dates, and I wanted to try this with you."

"The great Oliver Michaelson dating? Who would've thought?" I tease, sipping the alcohol while keeping my gaze on him.

"You're different, Chance. I'd like to get to know you. To delve into your mind and find out what makes you tick," he tells me earnestly. There's no playing around right now. Oliver's expression tells me all I need to know. He's made a choice, and now it's time for me to decide.

"Do I get to know what makes *you* tick?" I question. Bringing the glass to my lips, I watch and wait for the moment he realizes he can't hide from me. If I'm going to do this, there has to be transparency. I need to know about the man I'm getting into bed with.

"If you're a good boy, then yes," he smirks.

He fucking smirks.

An Adonis. There's nothing more perfect than his wolfish smile. I want to see it every day. More so than anything I've wanted before. Yes, the sex is amazing, it's mind-blowing, but there's something about seeing him carefree. Not lost in the darkness that sometimes clouds his eyes. I know many things are haunting him, and I plan to pull them to the surface and help him overcome whatever it is bothering him.

"Don't try to analyze me, Chance," he tells me then. "You'll fail." He rises to a full height, offering me his hand, which I gladly accept. He leads me into a dining room where the table is set for two. Plates have already been set out, and I wonder if he did all this. "I have a chef who came in to ensure everything is ready."

"You didn't have to go through all this trouble. I'd have been happy with pizza." My offered words cause him to chuckle. And that's the sound love is made of.

Love.

I wonder if Oliver will ever allow himself to feel it. To let in a person and show them everything. All the pain, all the heartache, and all the happiness.

"Sit." His command is low, a promise of what's to come.

Once we're both settled, he pours a glass of chilled water for himself and me. I know we're playing a scene tonight. At least, that's what he said. And I know for a fact he doesn't like to drink when he's in control.

"Do you ever lose control?" The question stills him and causes me to hold my breath. I don't know why I asked him, but I need to know. I wanted to learn about him, and this is the start.

"I did, a few times over the years. In a scene, out of a scene. There's always a time in everyone's life that control is overrated, or it's not needed for some reason."

I nod, sipping the water, mulling over what he's

said. I don't recall a time I'd let go of myself and let someone else take me, use me, allowing them the full power of my body.

"I've never hurt anyone . . . I mean." He smiles. "More than they needed. Chance, you have to understand, as a sadist, I enjoy the pain, doling it out."

"Yes, that much is clear. I just never thought of myself as a masochist, or even saw myself submitting to anyone."

He cocks his head to the side in awe, as if he didn't think about it until I said it. "Well, you're not completely submissive. You're also dominant," he explains, gesturing for me to eat. "That's called a switch."

Nodding, I can't help but moan at the flavors bursting on my tongue. The beef carpaccio is terrific, and I quickly finish the starter portion in front of me. We're silent as we eat, but I know there are more life lessons to learn tonight.

"It's not uncommon for someone to switch at times, or depending on the person you're with, different parts of your personality take precedence. I can never allow myself to submit. I . . ." His words taper off into a heavy silence. He shakes his head, then meets my inquisitive gaze once more. "I'm not submissive at all. I don't like allowing myself to be controlled by anyone."

"Is there a particular reason why?"

This causes him a wry smile. Sadness darkens his stormy eyes, and I wonder if he recalls a memory. "Let's just say, I've not always had control of a situation. But when I let it out of my grasp, there was pain. A lot of it."

"I'm sor—"

"Don't." The word is growled angrily as he pierces me with a thunderous glare. "Never apologize for something you didn't do or didn't have a hand in." He sets his cutlery down, then meets my gaze.

"Yes, Sir." I smile, attempting to lighten the mood, and for a moment, I think he's going to admonish me, but he doesn't. A mere nod is all I receive before he continues.

"My teenage years weren't perfect," he explains. "There were moments I wished I was dead. My father was never supportive of me, and my mother died when I was eleven, nearing my teenage years. But even though she left me, not by choice, I knew that she saw what my father was doing. Those are things I couldn't control. I lost a woman I could've loved, and my father got angry," he tells me.

I watch him swallow his water, then shake his head. I want to say something, to tell him that all parents can be assholes, but I don't. I allow him a moment to calm. He rises, makes his way through a door, and when he returns moments later, he's carrying two plates. It seems dinner is served when he places one in front of me and sets the other on his placemat.

"Tell me about your life."

"Uhm, well, I had both parents present all the time while I was growing up, and they were awkwardly supportive." I can't help but smile when I recall my mother fussing over me on my first date with a boy from school. We didn't call it a date, but that's what it was. I think she was more nervous than I was. "They didn't outwardly tell everyone about me, but when people asked, they wouldn't hide the fact that I would date both boys and girls."

"And Peyton?"

"She was the most understanding," I tell him with

a fond smile. "My sister is someone who will accept all your faults, shortcomings, and love you for who you are. But she knew before I told her. When I confessed, she practically leaped into my arms."

Oliver chuckles, and I know he can envision her doing just that. My sister is somewhat playful at times. And she certainly did love me no matter what.

"Yes, Peyton is a beautiful woman, right down to the heart and soul," Oliver muses. I know he cares for her. He's the one who got her and Carrick back together.

"I'd like to know something," I tell him, leaning my elbows on the table to pin him with a curious stare. When he gestures for me to continue, I do. "All these years, you've always been the one who gives everyone advice, helps others with their relationships, or their journeys in this lifestyle. Why is that? I mean, what about you? Don't you one day want a forever love as well?"

OLIVER

He's right.

I've always offered advice to everyone. I want to see people happy, but I never allowed myself to believe I could have that. Once, I did try to love someone. I focused on him. I let my mind drift back to the boy I thought I loved, but that wasn't the emotion I had envelop me.

"No," I respond finally. "I do find satisfaction in seeing my friends happy, seeing them live a life that's filled with love, but I'm not someone who can ever allow that emotion to take over me again."

"Again?" His brow quirks in response, and I know I'm talking myself into a corner. Chance is breaking through the walls I've built. I've perfected my cold, hard exterior for years, and one man seems to be cracking it.

"I was young and stupid. Not everyone who's around you has your best interests at heart," I tell him, cutting into the steak. I bring my fork to my mouth and meet his eyes as I pull the meat from the metal prongs. Chance's eyes are on me, attempting to read me, read my mind. He wants to know me, but I'm not sure if I'm ready to let someone in. Perhaps I am as broken as my father was.

"We were all young and stupid once." He smiles. "That's the beauty of life. We grow up, we learn, and we move on." His words are wise, sounding like something I would say. I can't help but smile at the young man. He's enamored me. "You've always given advice. I think it's time you take it as well."

"Oh?" I quirk a brow at him in question. "And you're the one who'd like to offer it to me?" I sip my water, waiting for his response.

"Maybe." I watch as he chews. His expression is pensive, and I wonder what's running around in his mind. I can imagine all sorts of questions he wants to ask but doesn't. Not yet anyway. Something tells me soon I will have to make a choice.

"Tell me something, Chance. Has anyone ever judged you unfairly? Or made you feel less *human* because of your choices?" This time it's me who takes a bite of my dinner as I regard him. His face looks like it's been chiseled by a sculptor. Sharp features, with deep-set green eyes. Full pinkish lips, with a perfect cupid's brow.

"Not to that drastic point, no." He sets the cutlery down and watches me for a moment. "I've had people sneer at me, and challenge my way of thinking or way of life, but not to the point where I feel less than human." He shakes his head, melancholy painting his features. "I think it's sad that anyone should live through that."

"And those who do tend to close themselves off to affection," I inform him, finishing his thought process. His gaze pins me for a long while as silence hangs in the air.

"Tell me, Oliver."

"People don't stick around long enough to hear my story, Chance. I've learned over the years to—"

"For God's sake," he bites out in frustration, causing me to smirk. When he's angry, frustrated, there's a fire raging in those gemstone eyes. A lock of hair falls over his forehead, making him look younger than he really is.

"That's the fire I love to see in my submissives," I tell him, dabbing the corners of my mouth with the napkin. "Now finish your drink, and we'll play a little game to get to know each other." Rising from my seat, I leave him at the table and make my way out toward the hallway. I know he'll follow, and when I hear footsteps behind me, I smile. Once I reach the door to my playroom, I twist the handle and shove it open. Flicking the lights on, I take note of how tidy it is — always hold onto control.

When Chance joins me, I allow him to take in the space. This is where he'll be tonight, enjoying whatever I decide to dole out. He moves around the area slowly, taking in every detail from the toys to the dark blue, silk sheets. The room is decked out in black, blue, and silver. There are toys along each of the walls, everything from whips to canes and butt plugs, which are displayed in glass cases.

"This is something else," he says, turning to face me. "It's almost regal, but only in blue, not purple."

Tipping my head to the side, I lean against the wall,

crossing my arms in front of my chest, and regard him. "You consider purple to coincide with royalty?"

He smiles. "Yes, I guess I do." Chance settles on the edge of the bed. Placing his hands on the mattress, he leans back and asks, "So, what are we doing in here?"

"I figured we'd have a scene. I want to see if you're ready to embark on your journey. I want to delve into your mind and find out what desires and fantasies are hidden in that handsome head of yours."

"That's not the only head that's handsome." He winks cockily.

"You're a smartass. Perhaps I should see how cocky you are once you've gotten a few lashes from one of my floggers, or perhaps you'd like to experience the bite of a cane."

His expression is thoughtful once more. "Perhaps you should teach me how to behave," he taunts with a wicked grin lighting his face.

"I can certainly do that," I tell him. Pushing off the wall, and I undo the cuffs of my shirt, which is still hanging loosely. "Take your shoes off, then your socks. Your slacks, followed by your shirt, then I want you on the bed."

He nods. "Yes, Sir." Immediately falling into the submissive role, he's perfectly obedient as he undresses in the order I've commanded him. It doesn't take long for him to be left in his briefs. They're tight, hugging his thighs and hips. The material does nothing to hide what I know is a delicious eight-inch cock.

Chance crawls up onto the bed. His body is slim, but he's toned in all the right places with a slightly defined stomach with a V-line that points to his groin. His arms are muscled, his forearms have a light dusting of golden-blond hair, just like the hair on his head.

He's pretty. Beautiful. And I wonder just how many men and women have gazed upon him, lost in his perfection. Just like I am now. He sits back on his heels, waiting for my next order. I'm already hardening just taking him in as he is in presentation pose.

"Lie back. I want to taunt you a little."

He smiles, positioning himself on his back. I make my way over to the cabinet and pull out the cuffs along with a blindfold. When I reach him once more, I proceed in binding him to the four metal posts of the bed.

"You're going to experience everything without sight. I'll tell you everything you'd like to know about me, but the trick is for you to ask the correct questions. What are your safe words?"

He smiles at my instruction. "Red to stop. Yellow when I'm nearing my limit," Chance rasps, and I know he's already hard. Before I bind his feet, I pull the briefs down his toned legs. His cock lies hard, pointing toward his belly button.

"Good boy."

I move to blindfold him next. Once he's ready, I take a step back and watch him for a moment. Perfect. Grabbing the matches, I strike one, lighting the bright red candle sitting on the nightstand. The flame flickers, and I'm reminded of how intense wax play is.

Tonight, Chance is going to learn just how broken I am. In an attempt to let someone into my heart, I'm going to allow him to see into my mind while blinded by material. When you want to love someone, when you're ready to say those words, seeing the person's soul is of utmost importance. And that's what I'm going to attempt this evening.

It's my first time, and I'm as nervous as I was the first time I felt a man's lips touch mine. Even though those memories bring along with them the pain of what happened, I close my eyes and breathe deeply for a moment before picking up the candle.

"Time to play."

CHANCE

The scent of candle wax invades my nostrils when Oliver nears me. I may not be able to see him, but I can feel him. There's a heat that emanates from the man, and I know deep down, he's blindfolded me so he can admit his pain. He may play the controlling Dominant, but I know Oliver's broken, and I realize the only way for him to be able to revisit his past is to do it without the attention on him.

"First question, Chance," Oliver says. His voice is low yet commanding. I'm about to respond when I feel heat trickling over my chest. It's not a lot, but a slight tingle, and then it's gone. The smell of wax, rose-scented, is in the air. My nipples harden. They're sensitive when he continues his delicious torture by allowing the hot liquid to drip onto each hardened bud.

"Tell me about your parents," I request in a whisper. My attempt at sounding calm flies out the window when my voice comes out husky, drenched in need.

"Interesting topic to begin with," he muses. "My mother died when I was eleven. I pushed the memories away, to cope with the pain of her no longer being there." The hot wax makes its way over my stomach, and it feels as if he's drawing the dips and peaks of my abs with it. The fragrance is even stronger now, and my cock is pulsing when I realize he's getting closer to my groin.

"And your father?" I urge, wanting to know more, needing him to focus on the story and not torturing me.

"He was an asshole. Still is, I guess. I haven't seen him in years, but he caught me with a classmate. We had kissed in the backyard of my childhood home." He traces his way down toward my thighs, just missing my cock by inches. "When he saw me, he lost his mind. How can the son of a high-profile lawyer be gay?" he utters with sadness lacing every word.

I think I've hit the nail on the head when he tells me this. Certain that's what broke him, I nod. "And that's why you're afraid to let people in?"

"I spent my life being bullied by him. Being told I wasn't good enough. I was a confused teenage boy who had a crush on his best friend. And then, said best friend left the school, and most of the friends he'd left behind found out what had happened. They learned who I was, or rather, what I was. They decided to bully me right through high school because I was different."

The sting is now on my other leg, my toes curling as pleasure mingles with pain shoots through me. My blood is boiling, both from the desire for Oliver and the need to avenge the assholes who hurt him.

"So, you were bullied. Ninety percent of kids are bullied," I tell him, hoping to offer him some form of confidence to allow me to look into his eyes, to see his pain and attempt to heal it.

"That's not a question."

"Fine. Tell me why you turned to sadism?" I shock myself with the question. I never thought of myself as a submissive, and I still can't explain my need to kneel for him, but I want to pleasure him, to offer him all of me, because he makes me feel whole. It's a strange emotion that seems to take hold when I'm around him. Is it love? I don't know yet. Perhaps it's too soon to tell, but I know I can love Oliver Michaelson.

"Pleasure is derived from pain," he informs me. "And pain comes from the acute pleasure of wanting something so much . . ."

His words taper off, and then I feel it. The sharp edges of a pinwheel. It tracks patterns over my skin, causing my hips to buck, my mind to lose all focus, and my cock to jolt wildly. He doesn't stop when I moan and grunt. The way it moves over my flesh causes my nerves to ignite with electricity that shoots through every inch of me.

I'm about to ask another question when he places it on my shaft. I've never cried out in pained pleasure like I do now. My throat burns as he draws paths over the underside of my shaft, stopping short of the tip. The sensitive area near the head is tingling, and all I want is his mouth on me.

"Please, Sir," I beg. I fucking plead because I need it.

"Please?" He quizzes me curiously. "Are you really that sensitive that you're ready to come?" This causes him to chuckle. He enjoys the torture; it's what gets him off. "How about we try one more?" He grips my cock so hard, and I lift my hips in an attempt to fuck his fist. "Oh no, you don't."

His hand leaves me, causing me to whimper in agony. My balls are tight, ready to release, but he's edging me. There's nothing I can do. I'm at his mercy, and Oliver is pleased.

Silence falls around me, and I can't tell where he is. He's certainly not near the bed. I can't feel his presence. Turning my head left and right, I try to focus, but I can't. I'm lost to the pleasure.

My body is trembling. I want to see, to feel him, but I can't move. It's then I hear it — a swish of a leather. Seconds later, I feel it. The lick of the flogger on my chest, on my thighs. He goes to town on me. Low grunts fall from my lips, but all I can focus on is each minor tail of the flogger lapping at my flesh.

"Are you done with your questioning?" he asks, clearly amused that I'm no longer worried about learning more about him, but rather my need for release. I can practically feel the welts rising on my legs, my stomach.

"I-I-I w-want t-to know w-who hurt you," I bite out. My attempt at sounding normal is pointless because my orgasm is teetering on the edge. It's peering down into the depths, and I'm about to come when he halts the lashing.

"What?"

The flogger falls to the floor. My blindfold ripped away, and the bindings that were holding me are gone in an instant. Oliver's body is visibly shaking, his cock — hard and thick — is prominent in his boxers.

"What did you ask me?" His hand is in my hair, tugging the short strands, pulling me closer to him. Our mouths are inches apart. The heat of his short breaths fan over my face and all I want to do is get lost in him.

"I asked you a question. Was that the right one?" I murmur.

His mouth crashes to mine. His tongue sweeps into my mouth, finding mine, and we dance in a duel of Dominance. I want more and yet he offers it. We're a mangled mess of limbs and mouths as his hands pull at my hair and the sting, bite of the strands being tugged cause me to wince.

"Tell me, Oliver," I finally utter when we break the kiss. My lips tingle, swollen from his violent movements.

"You will never find out," he vows. Shoving me backward, he kneels on the mattress. His hands land on my hips, flipping me onto my stomach. My cock is wedged between the mattress and me. Oliver rains down harsh swats on my ass, harder, and harder, and I wonder how his hand isn't hurting. The burn sends tingles through every part of me. My toes curl as pleasure takes precedence over the pain.

A moan falls from my lips, and that's when I feel it, cool liquid on my burning flesh. He opens me up to his invasion. I'm about to protest, to ask for forgiveness when he harshly shoves himself into me. A cry is torn from my throat, but he's no longer here. He's not in this room.

He moves fast, grunting behind me. I wonder if he's trying to really hurt me, and I can't help but call to him. "Oliver, please?" I turn my face, glancing at him over my shoulder. His steely gaze meets mine, and then he's back. The emptiness in his stare is gone, and the affection is here, slamming into me like a gale force wind, knocking the breath from me.

He pulls me up onto all fours, his one hand on my shaft, the other holding onto my hip. His body looms over me, and he continues fucking me while stroking me. My eyes roll back, and pain is replaced with pleasure, as I push back, fucking his cock into me.

I need this. I fucking crave it.

Oliver delivers violent thrusts as he jerks me off. His hand is moving so fast I can't stop the impending release trickling over me. I want to come for him, to offer him my orgasm.

"Give it to me," he growls. "I fucking own it. You want this, Chance? You want the monster?" he hisses in my ear as he plows deep into me. His cock pulses, thickens, and I know he's close, just as close as I am.

"Yes," is all I manage before I grunt out my seed all over his hand, the sheet below me, and I lose all sense of time when I feel Oliver lose himself in me. His hips piston once, twice, and a third time before he fills me in a low growl.

And I know for a fact I'll never be rid of this man.

He's inside me, more than physically. He's

burrowing his way into the very depths of my soul, and I can never get him out. Now, all I need is to find out what happened in his past.

OLIVER

The scent of freshly brewed coffee hangs in the air, and I know for a fact Chance has gotten up before me. The bed is empty, cold on his side, which makes me wonder how long he's been up. There's always a lingering fear that grips me when I have someone in my house. It's my personal space, the only place I know I'm in control. But with him here, wandering around, I've lost all sense of control.

Pushing off the bed, I head out toward the hallway and down toward the kitchen where I find him making breakfast. He's dressed in his briefs and nothing else. His tanned, toned back muscles work as he stands at the stove, frying up scrambled eggs.

"Are you going to stand there and stare at me, or

join me?" He turns to regard me, his green gaze meeting mine in playful curiosity.

"I didn't think you knew how to cook." I enter, settling myself on the stool, where Chance places a mug of steaming black coffee before me on the countertop.

"There are many things you have yet to learn about me, Oliver," he tells me but doesn't allow me to see his face. I know he's smiling; I can hear it in his voice. He sounds lighthearted, and I wonder if he's still thinking about last night. I made a mistake. I fucked up, and I need to apologize, but I've never lowered myself ever to say sorry to anyone.

"Well, it's best you tell me all about you." I sip my coffee, watching him as he plates the food, setting one piled high in front of me, and the other opposite, where he perches on a stool. His eyes sparkle with such playfulness I wonder if he'll ever confess his past to me.

"When I was sixteen, I noticed I was different, or I had different wants," he tells me between a bite of egg and bacon. When he swallows, he continues. "I wanted nothing more than to date a specific boy in my class. There was a longing inside me, wanting to be near him.

Of course, I wouldn't tell a soul. The private school was strict, and I kept my feelings to myself."

He smiles at the memory, and I know exactly what he means. But keeping so many emotions locked up can be a burden, and as a teenager, there are already so many things to think about.

"That's not something I can say is an easy feat. I know the feeling," I tell him, sympathizing with him.

Chance nods. "It certainly is not easy, but I'm thankful Peyton was there, and I could talk to her about it. What I needed to realize was that even though I didn't do what the other boys at school did — date high school girls, break their hearts, boast about fucking every girl in the school — I was still loved."

"And when did you realize you were bi?" I question after finishing my mouthful of food. It's delicious, but I don't tell him. I don't want to distract him from his story.

"After that date. I met a girl a year older than me. She was in town for vacation with her folks. We kissed, and I was ready to take things to second base. It was then I knew. When I confessed to Peyton, she smiled and shrugged as if it was the most natural thing in the world."

"She's a good woman, a good sister."

He nods with a broad smile. I know how she loves, with her whole heart. She doesn't allow anything to hinder how she feels. It's pure emotion, and that's something you don't see every day.

"Were there any low points? Not from your family, but others," I question, knowing this could be the moment he closes up, and when I lift my gaze to find his, I see burning in those emerald eyes.

"You really want to talk about this over breakfast?" he quips, covering up the pain so clear in his expression. "You know, Oliver, last night you weren't yourself. When I asked you—"

"This isn't about me, Chance." I set the mug down, pinning him with a serious stare. "This is about you. I told you what I could last night. There are many things for you to still learn about who I am, why I am closed off, but this is about you."

He sighs, lowering his stare to the counter. The fork he's holding pushes the food around on his plate, and I know he's trying to figure out how to tell me something dark, something that tortures him. One thing I've learned about Chance Moore is that he's as closed off as I am. He hides behind smiles and jokes. He plasters a fake grin on his face when he knows people can see through him, and it frustrates me more than I care to admit.

For years, I've stayed away from emotions and affection. I've focused on the scenes I played out, on the beautiful bodies I could mar with my whip and cane, but this kind of open conversation — what I'm doing with him — it's not something I'm used to.

As much as he may feel I'm being unfair or putting him on the spot, all I need to know is if he's as nervous about this as I am. A relationship wasn't what I was expecting when he walked into my office, or when he signed the contract. But this is where we are. Spending the night in my bed, breakfast the next morning. It's all so new to me.

"Oliver—"

"Chance, this is not part of what I've put in the contract, and to be honest, it's strange to get to know someone's innermost thoughts. If you were any other submissive, I would show you where the door is and go about my day without a second thought of you."

"Then why don't you?" he questions, straightening his spine as he regards me with a curious stare. I don't know how to answer him, because truthfully, I don't know myself.

"I want you here." My voice is husky, filled with a foreign emotion that doesn't make sense to me. But I allow it to keep me hostage, just for a moment. "I've never wanted anyone in my home before. This is my personal sanctuary, away from the everyday shit that I deal with. But for some reason, Chance, you've broken in, and I don't see a way of getting you out."

He smiles. There's a sadness to his expression, but also, there's a glint of something in those pretty green eyes that reminds me of expensive jewels. Chance shakes his head for a moment before speaking again.

"I was seventeen when I met a man. He was probably in his early thirties, handsome, rich, and he wanted me. He paid me to sleep with him." His confession chills me to the core. Yeah, I've done some questionable things in my life, and I may not be proud of any of them, but I would never take advantage of a young person like that.

"I thought I was special. He always made me feel that way."

This time, Chance chuckles darkly when he scoops more food onto his fork and puts it in his mouth. I watch him chew.

"Anyway, one night I went to his house. We were supposed to meet for some party. He told me his friends were interested in talking to me about my choices in college majors. These men were powerful, said they could get me a scholarship, and after my parents died, Peyton and I needed the help."

"Jesus." The word leaves my lips in a low, rage-filled hiss. "Please don't tell me you—"

"There were four of them."

"Give me a name," I bite out. He opens his mouth, but nothing comes out. I can tell he's warring with himself. "Chance, I swear on all that's holy, if you don't tell me—"

"James Hitchington."

That's all he has to say when I'm out of the chair, stalking down the hallway to my bedroom to retrieve my phone. I tap out a number and tell my contact to get back to me urgently. There's someone I need to find.

"You don't have to—"

"Yes, I fucking do," I bite out. "For my sanity and yours." My body is vibrating with the need to hurt someone, to find this asshole and show him just how fucking special he is. To rip into him and make him fucking bleed. I'll find him. I swear I will. When I turn around, I see those emeralds shimmering with sadness. And I know I'm fucked. I've fallen, and there's no way to get back up.

But do I want to?

CHANCE

I didn't expect to confess my darkest secret to Oliver. I didn't expect him even to care, but when he lost his shit and told someone to call him back, I knew he was on the warpath. He told me to stay at the house for the day, but I feel useless just lying around. I want to do something, to help him, but I was ordered not to leave the house until he calls.

Settling on the sofa, I flick on the television and stare blankly at the screen. I've always enjoyed mind-numbing TV, but this is ridiculous. The thought of not being able to leave has me on edge.

Picking up my cell phone, I hit dial on Peyton's number. She answers on the second ring, her voice raspy, and I'm certain I've woken her.

"Chance?"

"Hey, would you mind if I came over to your place?"

I hear her shuffling something, then a click of a door. "Yes, sure. Erin wasn't feeling well, so I've just sat with her until she fell asleep."

"I'll be over in a bit. Did you want me to bring anything?" I ask, already on my feet, excited to be able to leave the house for a little while.

"Just you, I have some wine or beer, and there's lunch as well," she tells me, and I can hear the smile in her words.

"See you soon," I tell her, hanging up and opening my messages. I know I'll have to let Oliver know, even though I'm not sure what we are to each other. I know if I disappear, he may lose his shit.

Tapping out a message to Oliver;

Chance: ***Going to see Peyton. I'll be back this evening.***

If he needs me, I'll be there, or he can call me.

Oliver: ***I trust you'll be home safely before I return.***

I can't help but smile at his gruffness. Even though he is adamant about affection being foreign to him, it's so clear he gives it in spades. But only in his unique way.

Chance: ***I will, Sir.***

Once I'm at my car, I quickly slip into the driver's seat and turn on the engine. Pulling out of the driveway, I weave through the midday traffic and head straight to Peyton's. Carrick bought a house just outside the city when the babies arrived. Even though they're no longer babies, I'll always see them as such.

I never pictured myself as a doting uncle. Kids were always a hindrance to me. Going out in public, I would avoid any place that would have children running around screaming. Now though, I love the girls. And I wonder if Peyton and Rick are planning any more.

Focusing on the road, I make it to their home in ten minutes, and as soon as I pull up to the gates, they slide open easily. I wonder if she's been watching out for me. The driveway isn't very long, and slowly, the two-story house comes into view.

Coming to a stop outside one of the garages, I kill the engine and exit the vehicle. Before I turn around to face her, Peyton's arms are around me, holding me hostage.

"Are you okay?" she questions, her voice muffled by my shirt.

After a moment to take in the silence and her embrace, she releases me, and I spin around to acknowledge her. "Of course I am. What's going on?"

She lifts her wide green eyes that match mine. "Oliver was here this morning. He was in a rage so fierce I thought he was going to break everything in the house. He almost punched a hole through the wall."

"What?" My voice sounds squeaky, foreign to my ears. "What do you mean?"

"He came to meet with Rick. They were talking, and I'd walked into the office as he was losing his shit. He spun around, almost punching the wall, but then he saw me and halted in shock."

Running my fingers through my unruly hair, I hiss, "Jesus." Stepping away from my sister for a moment, I watch her before continuing. "This morning, we had a little heart to heart. I told him what happened with James."

"Oh," she whispers. "Shit. I understand now." She laces her fingers with mine, tugging me into the house, through the entranceway, and into the kitchen. There are two steaming mugs of coffee waiting for us at the small kitchen table. Once we're seated, she fiddles with the handle of hers, not meeting my gaze.

"Peyton." Her name is a warning. I need her to tell me what Oliver did or said.

"He, Carrick, and Callan are out on a job," she mumbles, still not looking at me. I know she's feeling guilty about something because my sister is not the best liar, and when she is hiding something, she'll never look you in the eye. A tell-tale sign of hers I learned to read when we were growing up.

"And what job is this exactly?" I'm holding onto the mug, and even though I've asked the question, I know the answer. It's clear as day, right there in the air hanging around us. They've gone to find the man who hurt me.

Both love and fear mingle in my chest, gripping my heart so tight I'm not sure I'll be able to pull in a breath. I don't want Oliver getting involved in my past, but then again, the fact that he is tells me there's a lot more to this man than I thought.

If he can go out and hurt someone, then he's clearly

not just the upstanding businessman he portrays to everyone else. I always knew he held secrets, but he plays his cards so close to his chest I'm never sure if he's ever going to allow me to see them.

I know there's still something he's hiding from me. And I thought I could drag it out of him, but it seems it's going to take a lot more work than I'd initially anticipated.

"Look, Oliver has a business, and Callan helps him sometimes. They do undercover work," Peyton tells me, dragging me back to the present. "I . . . I don't know what it is, but there's a lot more to it than just finding missing people or scoping out secrets that some would prefer to hide."

"You mean he kills people?" A shudder rumbles through me at the thought of Oliver doing anything like that. Surely, there has to be an explanation for what he does.

"No, I just mean, I know Oliver is a good man. I wouldn't be okay with you dating him if he wasn't." She sighs, lifting those emeralds to mine. "I think there's much more to this story than meets the eye. I trust my husband, and he wouldn't do underhanded shit."

"I know." My response is a whisper as I place a hand on my sister's to confirm that I do not doubt her, or Carrick, or even Oliver. "I just need him to let me in."

"I thought you had a heart to heart this morning?" Her brow lifts in question, arching around her almond-shaped eye.

Nodding, I sip my coffee, which is slowly cooling down. "We did, but this is Oliver Michaelson we are talking about. Trying to get any information out of him is like trying to get water from a rock," I tease, hoping to ease the tension in the room.

Peyton smiles. The way her face lights up at the motion reminds me of why I had to watch her like a hawk through high school. Every boy in the building would follow her around like a puppy dog, wagging its tail hoping for a treat.

My sister is beautiful, classically so. Her sharp features, big green eyes, and long blonde hair are all perfection. She's filled out some since having the girls, but it only makes her more exquisite. She's a mom now, and I know she probably still has men staring at her.

Granted, I'm sure Carrick must scare them away. The man is rather possessive over his wife, and I don't blame him. I love how he loves her, with everything he has and is.

"Oliver is different," she says. "But just give him a chance. You never know how things will play out, and if this is meant to be, it will be."

"I know, sis. I'm just ready to take the next step, and I'm worried he's not. Correct that, I'm worried he'll never be." My honest response forms a lump in my throat.

"Have you admitted it to him?"

Shrugging, I shake my head no before meeting her shocked gaze. "I was scared. Honestly, he scares me just a little bit."

"He scares you, or are you scared he'll say no? Because Carrick does that to me, or he did when I realized I loved him. It's never easy admitting something like that to someone, especially when they're closed off to love, or affection, or anything resembling feelings, but if you never take the chance, you'll never know. Don't live with regrets, Chance, just do it."

"Yeah, yeah, now you sound like a Nike commercial."

She giggles. "And you love me for it."

"I do, sis, always."

I stalk into the empty living room knowing I'm alone in the house. The lights are still off, and Oliver's abrupt call telling me to meet him at his house has me more concerned and curious as to what was so urgent.

As soon as I left Peyton and Carrick's place an hour ago, my mind was on what Peyton and I spoke about. I drove around the city, killing time, trying to figure out how to come clean to Oliver and tell him how I feel. It's time to focus on what I want and admit that my feelings for him have changed.

I head into the bedroom, finding it empty, feeling weariness take hold of me. I want to take a nap, to be ready for him when he comes home. I have a feeling tonight may change everything between us. It might be good, or it might just cement the fear that's been sitting like a lead weight in my stomach for days.

It's time Oliver stopped hiding from me, hiding

from whatever is going on between us, and admit what he wants. If he can't tell me there could be a chance for us, I need to move on. I can't stay and fall deeper in love every day. Tonight, I will make sure nothing stands in the way of me getting into his heart and mind. Getting the truth out of him, and I also plan on getting his deliciously hard dick deep inside me.

The six-foot-three, lean-muscled God will finally face his fears and let me into his life. The click of the lock on the front door echoes through the house straight into the bedroom. I toe off my shoes, grab the lube, setting it on the side table, and hop on the bed.

"Chance." The deep, gruff rumble of Oliver reverberates over the silence, sending heat coursing through my veins. I'm ready. I'm hard. And I'm going to make sure that Oliver never forgets tonight.

"In here," I call out.

Once the man who's stealing every part of me saunters into the bedroom, his tie undone, the top three buttons of his shirt loose offering me a glimpse of skin beneath, I can't help licking my lips.

"You look exhausted," I tell him, rising from his bed

and making my way over to him.

"Been a long day," he growls, his hands gripping the shirt I'm wearing and tugging it free, causing buttons to fly in every direction.

"We need to—"

"Talk after. I need to release some tension." The depth with which those words vibrate through me has me nodding wordlessly. A smirk lifts his full lips — they're dusty pink, curled perfectly, which only makes me lick my lips hungrily.

"I have an idea." I grin, waiting for him to move. The room is filled with sexual tension so thick and heavy my lungs struggle to take in breaths. "I figured we could shower together," I continue when he doesn't say anything. Stepping back, I wait for him to make the next move. I've made my offer. It's time for him to come to me.

Slowly, I shrug off my shirt. He watches as my pants hit the floor and I step out of them. I don't have socks on, so I'm only dressed in a pair of tight, dark briefs.

He narrows his stormy gray eyes at me with a dark brow arching in question. "And you're waiting for me to say no?" He gestures, toeing off his black shoes. Once he's dressed in only his dark boxers, I can't help staring at him. He's nothing short of an Adonis.

"I was," I affirm, crossing my arms. I smile when he shakes his head and chuckles. The sound is one I'd like to hear over and over again. We're almost the same height; both broad shouldered with lean muscles. Keeping in shape is something I've always prided myself in. And when I look at Oliver, I know it's all worth it.

His gaze devours me. Like a feral fucking animal, he looks at me like I'm his last meal. "Where were you today? I was worried." My words are filled with need, with the desire to learn more about this intriguing man.

He sighs, walking toward the bathroom with me following hot on his heels. I watch him turn on the shower, the spray hissing, hitting the cool blue tiles that adorn the room.

When he doesn't speak, I take it as my chance to finally admit all the shit that's been building up over the past few days. "Listen, you know I want you, Oliver. There's no doubt in my mind you feel the same. Why do you keep pushing me away?" I sound like a fucking pussy, but I need to know. He needs to decide what he wants.

He turns, shooting daggers at me with those devilishly sexy eyes. "You know what, Chance? This is ridiculous. I didn't come home for this shit. I told you, we'll talk later."

"This shit . . ." I gesture between us. "I don't want 'this shit' between us. If you want this, we're both men. Fucking act like it," I grunt out, unsure of where the courage came from, but I'm done playing his games.

He pivots, shoving his boxers down his thick thighs. He's all man. Hard, ready, and it makes my mouth water. When I meet his cool-gray eyes, I find anger and lust swirling through them. Both emotions slam into me, and in two strides he's pressing his body against mine.

With a tug, he drags me into the shower. I'm slammed against the wall, my face flat on the tiles. His chest to my back and he rolls his hips, allowing me to feel his hard cock ready to rip into me like I've never had it before. "You want this?" he whispers along my ear. "Because I'll fuck you so hard right now that you'll need a fucking stretcher to get out of this shower."

I grunt, groan, then push back against him. My ass rubbing on the thick shaft throbbing with need against me. A feral hunger to let him fuck me deep and hard burns through me, and I'm breathless at the thought.

He reaches for me. Gripping my wet, unruly hair, he tugs it back so his mouth is right at my ear again. "You see, Chance, this is what you do to me." He groans as he rolls his hips again, his cock nestled between my ass cheeks. "I'm going to fuck you in this shower. I'm going to be so deep inside you, and you're going to remember me every time you move."

The shower has misted everything around me, and everything seems foggy. Our bodies are slick and wet. He releases me and turns me to face him. I allow a smirk to curl my lips, meeting his gaze in a challenge. "You better get to it then. I'm not waiting forever."

I watch him step under the spray, the water cascading down his tanned skin. My gaze greedily devours him as he grabs the bottle of soap, squirting some in his palm. Once he works it into a lather, he rubs it over his body, causing my cock to jolt in response.

The white suds trickle down his torso, only makes

me impossibly harder. When I step in closer to him, he hands me the soap, and we both take turns taunting each other with our touches, ignoring the rigid cocks so hard they could break glass.

"Suck my dick," Oliver grunts, his hand stroking the thick, angry erection. Dropping to my knees, I glance up at him. The smirk he loves to gift me with is present on his handsome face. Once all the soap is rinsed off his dick, I take it in my mouth, swallowing it deep into my throat.

The animalistic growl that echoes from him is more than enough to spur me on.

"Shit, yes," he hisses through his teeth. "Take that fucking dick." His voice is low, husky. He sounds like a fucking caveman. His fingers tangle in my hair, holding my head steady while he fucks my mouth deep and hard. "This what you wanted?" He bites out the question between pleasured moans. I can't nod. I can't do anything but allow him control. "Jesus Christ, yes. Fucking take it all." He bucks his hips faster and faster, and then his body locks. His orgasm shudders through him as he shoots jet after jet of hot release into my mouth.

OLIVER

I watch as Chance licks his lips of my arousal. His green eyes peek up at me under those golden lashes, and they seduce me more, pulling me into his orbit. It's only been seconds since I emptied myself into his mouth, but I already want more.

"I had a man taken care of today," I utter, offering him more of me than I've ever given anyone. "And I did it for you. Because of you."

Chance rises to his full height, his eyes burning into mine, searching for my soul. I've hidden away for so long, held the darkness inside me at bay, but for some reason, Chance brings it out and makes me want to lay myself bare.

It's unsettling.

It's unnerving.

And I'm unsure of what to do from here.

"You went to find him. Didn't you?"

"Well." I smile, pulling him closer, planting a kiss on his lips. "I had contacts find him. He was living in Miami." My voice lowers. "And what he did to you, he's done to many more since you. So, I trust that you're not feeling sorry for the asshole who is soon to be six feet underground."

He shakes his head slowly, but he doesn't respond. I wonder if he's sad about the turn of events, but then he leans in close, his body pressing against mine, which only makes me want more of a connection. It's new to me as there's a certainty in the way he moves. His self-assured confidence has my cock straining.

As the hot water cleanses us, he runs his hands up and down my back, eliciting a groan from deep in my throat. Jesus, this man is going to break me down into tiny pieces. His lips feather along my neck, and his cock jolts against me.

"Take me," I tell him. Finally giving him the one thing I haven't given anyone in years. Chance steps back; his brows furrow in confusion. "This is your choice now. We're either in this forever, or we're not in it at all."

I step away from him, turning with my back to the man who's broken through every barrier and learned some of my darkest secrets, but still hasn't left.

"Oliver—"

"Fuck me. I need it." My voice is husky, drenched in the desire to feel wanted. Needing the affection, I realize only Chance can give this to me. I press my hands on the tiles and wait. I feel his body cocoon me, his cock at my ass.

His hands massage me as he reaches for the tube I've handed him. He palms the cheeks of my ass, opening me to his hungry gaze, and his fingers tease me with the slick liquid.

Gently, he moves one finger into my opening, in and out, causing me to groan and my cock to jolt. He inserts a second digit and works me open, scissoring me to loosen the muscle. I need this. I realize it as he nudges a third finger into me, and I can't stop the rumbling grunt that escapes my lips.

"Do it, Chance. Just fuck me. I want it."

His fingers disappear. The tip of his cock replaces them, and soon, he's sliding into me. Everything turns to black as I shut my eyes and savor his thickness. A shudder of pleasure races through me when I feel the ridges of his shaft, the warmth of his hands on me, and his lips at my neck.

"Jesus, Oliver," he hisses in my ear. "I don't know how long I can last." His brutal honesty makes me smile. I don't think I can last because my cock is steel, ready to release another load on the tiles before me.

"Move. Just move." My command is bit out in a low grumble, as he moves. His hips move back, then slide forward, fucking me deep. His balls slap against mine. The sensation is mind-altering as I tense, feeling my orgasm trickle down my spine.

His hands are on my cock, stroking me faster and faster, mimicking his movements inside me. I know I'm tightening around him already, attempting to milk his cock of every drop of seed he has.

Our groans and grunts are the only sounds I focus on. Not even the spray of the shower can overpower the feral, animalistic noises. Our bodies move together, back and forth, in and out.

"Oliver—"

"Come for me, Chance. Obey me and come," I growl through clenched teeth as I try to focus on holding mine off for a second more, but once I feel his heat, I can't hold back. My cock spurts in his hands; jets of white seed paint the tiles and trickle down the drain.

"Fuck." His word is bit out as we both tremble against each other. I've never felt anything as sensually erotic as Chance's cock filling me. I can't breathe for a moment. My focus is on the way my heart seems to catapult in my chest at what I've just experienced.

He softens, slipping out of me, and I know that won't be the last time we do that. When I finally turn to face him, I grip the back of his neck and pull him in for a kiss. Our mouths fuse, tongues dancing against the other as we lick and taste, savoring the flavor of each other.

When I finally pull away, I meet his green stare. "Now it's time for us to talk. Okay?" He nods. I know he was expecting me to say something else, but it's not the time for that. Honestly, I don't know when the time will come. "Let's get out of here and dry off."

I step out of the shower, feeling the disappointment in Chance's eyes as he watches me, but I don't look at him. There are things to discuss, and that's more important right now.

In the living room, I focus on him as he fidgets. He's nervous about what I'm about to say, and I don't blame him. The silence that hangs heavily around us is deafening.

"The men informed me they had found that asshole, and he's done. He won't be hurting anyone else. Now, my question to you is, are there any other secrets lying in that pretty head of yours?"

His gaze snaps to mine. "No. I told you everything about my past, not like your bullshit excuse of not wanting me to know about your darkest secrets."

"Don't take that tone with me, Chance."

"Why? Because you're going to whip me?" he bites back in frustration, and I have to say, I'm proud of him for standing up for his wants and needs.

Sighing, I rise and stalk over to the bar. Pouring us each a drink, I gulp mine down before I head over to him and hand him the glass. "I never once told you this was more than a contract. Before you agreed—"

"Before I agreed, you were the one who let me in. Inch by inch, you allowed me to see you, the real you, and I'm not sorry if I want to know more."

"I understand. I messed up." Nodding, I take my seat and watch him drink the alcohol. "As I said to you before, I don't do relationships. I'm not inclined to want that."

"So, you'll never collar someone? Own someone?"

"No." I shake my head. "I don't want that life. I enjoy having multiple partners, training both men and women. I love the variety that comes with exploring."

"What if someone wanted that with you?" His question stills me, shocking me silent. "I mean, what if you found a person who would enjoy that promiscuity with you?" I'd never once considered something like that. A polyamory-type of relationship. Would it work? Perhaps. But I don't know if I could let myself love. And that's what Chance wants. I can see it in his eyes each time he looks at me. That gentle pleading in his gaze that begs for affection I'm incapable of giving someone so close to me.

"Are you saying you'd consider an open relationship?"

"It's not a hard limit." He smiles, and I know he's trying to lighten the mood. "It could be fun." Another offering that makes me rethink everything for a moment.

"I don't know. Chance, this life—"

"Oliver, just think about it. Please." He sets the glass down, shrugs on his jacket, and glances at me once more. "I'm going home. I'll see you tomorrow with Cayleigh."

"You know she's going to leave us," I offer before he turns to walk out of the living room and out of my house. "She's not built for this relationship scenario you're suggesting."

"I know. She was going to leave before this. But she's not the one I'm asking to leap with me. It's you. She may not be built for it, but are you?" With that, he turns and leaves me to ponder my thoughts. And the question burns in my mind. *Am I built for it?*

OLIVER

It's been eight hours since Chance walked out of my house. And every second that ticked by reminded me why I didn't want a relationship in the first place. He's under my skin. He's everything I want, and I don't know how to deal with it.

Yes, I've spent my life offering advice to others, making sure my friends were happy. Seeing them live out their own happily-ever-afters gave me the freedom to live vicariously through their smiles and laughs. But deep down, I knew it would never be enough. And as much as I knew that, I'd never met someone who made me want my own happy ending.

Until Chance.

My phone rings shrilly, dragging me out of the

thoughts of him.

"Oliver Michaelson, how can I help you?"

"Mr. Michaelson, this is Dr. Forester," comes the voice on the other end of the line. "I'm afraid I have some bad news."

Before he tells me, I already know. I swallow back the lump in my throat and nod to no one in particular. "Okay?"

"He's not doing so well. Your father doesn't have long, Mr. Michaelson. I would suggest you come to say your goodbyes." I don't respond because I can't. It's been years since I thought I would ever get this call, and even though I knew he was sick, deep down I thought he would live forever.

"Yes," I respond finally. "I'll see what I can do." I hang up before he can say anything more as shock slowly seeps through me. At forty-five, I can't believe I need to say goodbye to my father. To the man who made me the cold, heartless asshole I am today.

My body vibrates with confusion and pain. I don't know why I feel the agony lancing my chest, but I do. Perhaps it's because I have no way of calming myself down.

Picking up my phone, I hit dial on the number for Hayley, who's one floor down working in accounts. She's known me for almost a year, and she won't be shocked if I call her up here for a harsh spanking.

"Mr. Mich—"

"My office. Now."

Hanging up, I rise and pull my belt from its loops. I wrap it around my fist and wait for her to enter my office. The soft click of heels alerts me that someone is at my door. As soon as it flies open, I find the beautiful blonde on the threshold.

"Come in, shut the door, and bend over the desk." My order causes her eyes to widen in shock, but she doesn't disobey or question. I watch with a smirk when she lifts her skirt, bending to my will.

Rounding the front, I grip her panties in one hand and tug harshly, ripping the material from her hips. A soft squeak falls from her lips, which allows me to focus. With the belt wrapped around my fist, I raise my hand and bring it down on her supple ass.

It's beautiful watching her creamy flesh turn red.

The bright welt becomes a shade of lovely rose. It's as if there were a flower blooming on her ass, and I can't stop my hand bringing down more harsh swats on each cheek.

Her whimpers and mewls calm me, and I focus on the here and now, not the anger flowing through me. The rage I feel for my father not being there for me my whole life, but instead, more concerned about women and money.

The echoes of the leather on her creamy skin fill my office, reminding me I'm here. I'm in control. My breathing is ragged, and my chest is aching as I drop the belt.

"Stand." My voice is a husky grunt, and the gorgeous woman rises to face me. Her knees wobble from her spanking, and her eyes shimmer as pleasure trails through her.

"Thank you, Sir." She smiles, her cheeks burning red with need and embarrassment. I don't respond, merely help her right the skirt she's wearing and send her on her way.

Flopping onto my office chair, I close my eyes and

try to calm the raging hard-on in my slacks. The news of my father has hit me straight in the gut. And I know I'll need to decide if I'm going to go back to the shithole town I grew up in, or if I'm going to let him die alone.

My office door opens an hour later, and I glance up to find Cayleigh at the threshold. I crook my fingers to invite her in. Once she shuts the door, she strolls to the chair opposite my desk and perches her pert little ass on the cushion.

"How are you, darling?" I smile, trying to sound light-hearted, even though I don't feel it. Not with everything riding on my choice.

"I need to talk to you." I knew she needed this. Cayleigh may enjoy her submission and the lifestyle, but she's made for another man who can offer her the things every girl dreams about. She needs her knight in shining armor, and I know as much as she's enjoyed her scenes with us, and with me, she needs more.

"You know I'm always there for you, darling. What can I do for you?"

"Have you ever been in love?" Cayleigh's voice is tentative. She's still as shy as she was the day she walked into my office the first time. I like it.

I watch her for a moment, trying to gauge where she's going with this. Then I shrug, shaking my head. "No. I learned that love is merely a distraction from life." My words are honest. More so than I've ever voiced to anyone. It's true. "I focus on the here and now, not what's coming in five or ten years. Love is an emotion that doesn't come into play in my life. I prefer doling out pain to those who beg me for it."

"That's not true," she argues. "Love is freeing. It allows you to be yourself with someone who accepts you as you are." She's adorable when she's adamant about something.

Shaking my head, I rise and stalk toward the window. The city below us is alive with possibility, and I wonder just how many people down there are currently having their heart broken.

"When I was a teenager, I knew I was different," I tell her without looking into her eyes. I don't want her to see what I always hide from everyone around me.

The pain. The agony of having yourself torn in two by people you trust. "I accepted it. If I'm brutally honest, I was proud of the fact that I found my passions early on in life."

"Not many people can say that," she says, and I can hear the smile on her face. The pretty girl who's enamored me. "I . . . I just wonder if . . ." Her words taper off, and I watch her in the window. The slightly rippled view of her is what I focus on. It's been years since my training has taken me on an emotional path. She stays silent as she slowly rises. I expect her to come toward me, but she doesn't. I can see her reflection in the glass, and I wonder just what is going through her mind.

"Friends and family didn't want me to be different. My father, a lawyer, wasn't impressed that his only son was bisexual." Even now, years later, it still stings when I admit how much my father hated me, how his disappointment in me shattered my world. I spent my life trying to be the perfect son, and I let him down.

And when I walked out, I didn't look back. Knowing he's dying is something I didn't ever let myself think about. Children always think their parents will be there forever. That those parents would live long enough to age with them into those difficult teenage years, or even watch as they grow up, becoming adults.

"There's nothing left for me in that home. He's dying, and I can't feel anything. The man was disappointed in me since the moment he realized I would never be like him. He believed my sexuality was a vice, something that needed rectifying, but you cannot change who you are for someone else."

"Oliver, I'm—"

"Don't," I bite out in frustration. This is the reason I don't tell anyone about my life. Pity is something I despise, and when someone looks at me with that particular emotion, I feel weak.

I promised myself a long while ago I'd never be weak again, and I intend on keeping my promise.

"But—"

"Cayleigh." Her name is a warning on my lips, causing her to shut the fuck up. I don't need a reminder of what a mess my past is. I don't even need to know why I'm so broken inside. I've had enough of those memories to last a lifetime. "He's dying. I don't care. Is that what you want to hear? My father has been the ruler of my life for as long as I can remember. Even when I walked out of my childhood home, he was there, berating me for my choices. Yes, he paid my way, but . . ." I shrug, not wanting to continue this tirade.

Forgiveness is not something I've come across throughout my life. And with the one man who's dying, I can't find it in my heart to offer it to, but I know I need to make a choice.

"You can't let your parents rule your life." Leigh smiles sadly. "If those who are closest to you cannot accept you for who you are, then it's their loss." She's right. "But if he's dying, Oliver." Her words have turned into a mere whisper. I can hardly hear her, but it's as if she's right in my ear, in my head, telling me exactly what I need to hear.

I want to nod. I want to agree with her and offer her the acknowledgment my father couldn't give me, but I don't. Sighing, I unbutton my cuffs and roll up my sleeves. Once they're at my elbows, I fist both hands. I didn't call Cayleigh here for a heart to heart. We were meant to play a scene in the office, but I find myself unfocused. And I never enter a scene with anyone if I'm not there one hundred percent.

My body is rigid. I've never told anyone about this. Never allowed anyone into my mind like she's slowly delving into it. Bit by bit, Cayleigh O'Leary is just like her brother Carrick. They want to help. In their own way, they push until there's no choice but to give in. Her words cause me to turn around. Finally, I face my new submissive, a beautiful soul who has entrusted her body with me. The only person missing is Chance. If he were here, I have a feeling he'd say the same thing.

"So, you're telling me that you have never found love?" she continues in her sweet way as she watches me. But I'm tired of rehashing my past. It's time to see how well she's learned to control herself with me.

Before I close this topic completely, I meet her burning stare with my hardened gaze and offer my response. "You can't find what you don't look for," I tell her. My gaze darts between Leigh and my desk where I'm tempted to bend her over, whip her until she's mewling, and her porcelain flesh has welts. "Now, enough emotional shit. Tonight, I want you at my house.

Chance will be there, so I hope you'll be ready to take us both."

"Yes, Sir," Cayleigh murmurs as she steps forward, closing the distance between us. "Please don't shut us out for what *he* did to you."

I smile. It's a sad one as it doesn't reach my eyes. I wish I could allow people into my heart. How I wish I could love them, both of them. I may enjoy their bodies, their desire, but I can't love. I've tried, but it's not possible. This is why I've become the cold monster I am right now.

"Tonight, meet me at eight," I tell her before returning to my seat. "Now, get out of my office, and if anyone hears about what happened here today, you won't be able to sit down for a month. I'll cane your pretty little ass, then fist your tight holes until you're nothing but a mess, pleading for me to stop. Am I understood?"

"Of course, Sir," she says, but I can tell she's burning to bite out a snarky comment or retort, something that will earn her the cane on her thighs and ass.

I watch as Cayleigh strolls from the office and leaves me to think about what she said. The call I got this morning was enough to leave me confused and hurting. But I don't allow any emotion to show. It's been years since I laid eyes on my father, and the moment the doctor told me he doesn't have long, I knew I had to make a decision.

Sighing, I sit back and allow my thoughts to linger on what to do. If I were to walk back into his house, look at him frail and broken, it may have been something I wanted years ago when hate and anger were all I knew. But now . . . I guess I may want to finally hear my father tell me he's somewhat proud of me.

Perhaps even give me some semblance of a goodbye, closure, or even, god forbid, he tells me he doesn't hate me. But that's something I know will never happen. With the rage he spewed the moment I turned seventeen, I knew there would never be any love lost between us.

My whole adult life I've spent moving on, focused on work, on my sexual needs, and on the fact that I'll never bring a child into this world. Not because I don't want to be a father, but because I never wanted to be *him.*

CAYLEIGH

Glancing in the mirror, I take in the floor-length black dress I bought earlier today. The slit slides all the way up to my thigh, and the back is scooped down to the base of my spine. My cleavage peeks out, offering a glimpse of my breasts.

Tonight, I'll finally say goodbye to the two men who brought me back to life. It might sound overly dramatic, but it's something I've thought about, and I know if it weren't for the chance I took with Oliver, I wouldn't be able to admit what I want, or what I need.

Slipping on heels, I grab my purse and head for the door just as the bell alerts me the driver Oliver sent is here. He sent a message only an hour ago to let me know he'd prefer having someone collect me than have me drive alone.

"Ms. O'Leary." The man in a penguin suit offers me a slight nod.

"Hello." I'm nervous. I'm not sure why, there's nothing for me to worry about, but still, my stomach is filled with a million butterflies awake, fluttering around.

The driver opens the door, waiting for me to settle on the backseat of the Bentley. As soon as he's in the driver's seat, the engine purrs to life, and we're making our way toward Oliver's home.

Watching the city pass by, I wonder what it would be like living in Los Angeles. I've asked Eva if she and Nathan would put me up for a little while. Thankfully, they've both offered me a guest room for as long as I need.

Everything will be new. I'll be away from my brothers, and I'll finally be able to be independent even though I know for a fact that Carrick and Callan will never just let me live there without checking up on me every day. But they won't be in the same city, and that makes me grin.

I've never lived on my own, always had someone

there, and I know I need to experience it. Stepping out into the world, I'm going to need to focus on who I am as a person finally. Not a sister, not a daughter, and certainly not a fiancée anymore.

My heart still aches at times when I think of Sean, but the past can never be changed, so I need to move on. And that's why I know a fresh start is the only way I'll be able to put the murder behind me.

The car pulls up the drive and stops outside the door, which is slightly ajar, and I wonder if Oliver's left it that way because he knew I was on my way. The car door opens, and I step out onto the paving. Taking in my surroundings, I notice how beautifully manicured the garden is. Even with the yellow lamps that trail their way up the driveway, I can make out quite a lot of the nearby land.

"There she is." Oliver's voice comes from the doorway, causing me to cast my glance his way. He's dressed in dark slacks and a white shirt. His salt-and-pepper hair is stylishly messy, and there's a light dusting of stubble along his jaw.

"It's good to see you again." I blush, remembering

our last scene. Even though we spoke about it, I still can't get it out of my mind. How he lost control, but also, how much I loved every moment.

"Come inside. Chance is here already." He offers a nod to the driver, and his fingers find the base of my spine as he leads me into the large entrance hall. The tiles are white, almost glassy, as the walls are a stark contrast in their charcoal appearance.

"This is incredible," I tell Oliver as he leads me farther into the house. Elegance, class, and style seep from every corner, and I'm not surprised. Oliver is one of those men who exudes wealth and confidence, but he also emanates affection. Perhaps he doesn't see it or even admit it, but I've come to learn he's got a soft heart.

"Thank you." He sounds proud of my awe. When we enter the living room, Chance turns to regard me. His green eyes shimmer like gemstones in the soft yellow lights hanging from the center of the room. A crystal chandelier that's not bawdy, but rather elegant, hangs low into the room, offering warmth even though there are high ceilings.

"Hi, darling." Chance leans in to press a kiss to my

forehead. He pulls me into his arms, holding me for a moment, almost as if he knows this will be the last time I see him. I plan to fly out in a couple of days, and tomorrow I'll be packing and arranging my transport to the airport.

"You're looking rather dashing," I tease, tugging on his shirt, which has the top three buttons undone. His hair is normally styled perfectly, but at the moment, it's tousled as if someone has been tugging on the strands. "Did you start the party without me?"

"Perhaps." He grins playfully, and I know there's something more going on between them. I'm beyond pleased Chance has finally broken through to the older man.

"I need to tell you both something before we go any further." My voice is filled with emotion that causes tears to prick my eyes.

They both watch me, waiting for my admission. I've found who I am, what I want, and it was all thanks to Oliver and Chance. But I know I don't love them in that way. I doubt I could, even if I spent more time around them.

"I've decided to move out to Los Angeles to stay with Nate and Eva for a while," I finally utter. It feels as if I'm breaking up with someone, but they're not my *someone*, and we all know it. For a while, it was fun, but it's time they found the love that's so clear between them.

"Are you sure?" Oliver rises, stalking toward me. He grips my arms, holding me close, and I nod. "I'm never one to stop someone from finding themselves, so I wish you all the happiness in the world." He smiles, giving me that handsome grin that lights up his steel-gray eyes, which seem to penetrate every secret inside me.

"Thank you, Oliver. I don't know if I could've gotten here without you. I've never been strong enough in my own choices to do the things we've done," I tell him honestly. It's true. I've always hidden my needs from people, but it's time to stop that. I'm old enough to know if people don't like who I am, they can move along and leave me to live my life the way I want.

"And you're going to tell Carrick and Callan?"

"Yes," I affirm with a nod. "It's time for me to get out from under the shadow of my family, of my brothers, and it's time for me to explore."

"Remember you have safe words. If you need me, if you need anything," Oliver tells me with the seriousness of a father sending his child off into the world.

"I know. I'll call on you if need be, but I think I'll be okay."

"You will." He steps back, allowing Chance to near me. He pulls me into a hug so fierce I feel my lungs fight for air. He's one of the sweetest men I know, and I love him, but he's a good friend who I know a little more intimately than I expected. It's not a bad thing at all, but I know he's not the one who holds my heart either.

"I'm going to miss you, baby girl," Chance tells me with sadness dripping off every word.

"Would you like a drink, Cayleigh?" Oliver offers, dragging my attention to him for a moment, and I nod.

"Yes, please. Just a white wine."

Oliver leaves us for a moment. I guess he's heading to his kitchen when I take the opportunity to impart some wisdom on the man who's become one of my best friends.

"Tell him, Chance," I hiss, cupping his cheeks in my

hands. "You need to tell Oliver how you feel about him before he walks away."

He tries to shake his head, but I hold it steady.

"I'm serious. Do it. Promise me," I urge him, and I know if he makes a promise, he can't break it. "Please."

"Okay, okay," he sighs, rolling his eyes. "I promise." His words are uttered in frustration, but I'm happy because I know he'll follow through. "But if it all falls apart, I'm blaming you."

"Oh please. You two eye-fuck each other all the time. But it's not even that. He looks at you like you've hung the sun in the sky." Leaning up on my tiptoes, I press a kiss to Chance's lips before I step back, knowing they'll always be there for me, no matter what. My life awaits, and I realize I need to talk to Rick and Callan before they lose their shit.

"Dinner?" Oliver offers when he returns to the room. Chance and I nod, and Oliver leads us into a dining area. I can't help smiling that the last meal I'll have to remember with them is knowing Chance will finally admit his feelings. Now I only hope Oliver opens his eyes to see what's right in front of him.

CHANCE

The dinner with Cayleigh was lovely, and somehow, I knew it would be a friendly one. There wasn't any tension or even animosity about her leaving. She knew how I felt about Oliver, and I'm thankful for that.

I'm proud of her for going after what she wants. Focusing on her life and not being scared of stepping out of the shadow of her brothers. Sighing as I make my way upstairs, I realize my exhaustion is due to Cayleigh making me promise I'd tell Oliver how I feel. I don't know how though. As soon as I mention anything about emotions, feelings, he closes up and pushes me away.

The room is dimly lit when I enter, and I know he's sleeping, or at least faking it. Staying over has been a strange, moot point. After our scenes, I've settled on the sofa and fallen asleep, but now I'm here, in his bedroom, a place not many people have been lucky enough to enter, and I don't know how to handle it.

He's always made me feel welcome, but deep down, I wonder if I'm invading his space. Settling on the chair at the window, I watch the city twinkle below us, wondering what the people are doing as they go about their business. All my life I've been a people watcher, and even now, I find it intriguing seeing how people move around each other, interact, or even just sit on their own.

"Are you coming to bed? I'm tired, and I need to be up early in the morning." Oliver's deep voice sounds like a beacon from the bed in the night. I don't look at him. Keeping my gaze on the window, I sigh.

"I was just wondering if you wanted me there," I tell him, feeling far too emotional for this. Whenever I was in a relationship in the past, I was always in charge, but this is all foreign territory for me. He's been off all night. Even though he was friendly at dinner, talking to Cayleigh about her upcoming trip and what she's going to do in LA, I know something is bothering him.

I want to delve into his mind, just like he does with every submissive that crosses his path. To dip into the darkness so clearly haunting him. I want to draw it out and light a way for him to find happiness. Not the happiness he fakes with everyone. I want a real smile, a laugh that warms me inside. To see those stormy eyes clear for once, and see them shimmer with light.

"I wouldn't have you in my house, in my bedroom, if I didn't want you here, Chance." He sounds tired, and I know something is troubling him. He slowly scoots up in bed and sits there in the dark. "I'm leaving tomorrow," he tells me suddenly. This has come out of nowhere.

"What?"

"I have things to do, and I'll be driving up to my hometown to sign some papers, say goodbye to the shithole, and never look back." His voice is icy, but there's a sadness to it—something I'd never seen Oliver express.

"Why? What are you going to do there?" I move across the room and perch on the edge of the mattress, watching him in the dark. He's drenched in darkness, and he seems at home there.

"My father is dying, and I need to go sort his shit out," he expresses emotionlessly. All the sadness I thought I heard moments ago is gone. I thought he seemed tenser today, but I didn't realize he has this weighing on him. "It's inconvenient when I have work to do here, but there's not much time apparently." The venom in his tone tells me there's so much more to this story than he's letting on.

"I'm guessing there will be a lot to do there."

"Yeah," he responds, raking his fingers through his hair, not meeting my stare in the darkness. He's closed off. Shut himself out from the world, and I'm part of that world. My heart cracks with every word.

I want to hold him, tell him it will be okay, but I know that's not what he needs. Oliver is a man who wants tough love. So, I don't say *I'm sorry,* or *I'm here for you.* Instead, I sit and watch him in the darkness.

When your parents are dying, it's never easy to push it aside and steel yourself from the pain of knowing they're no longer going to be around. Even if they didn't get along, there must be some heartache that's bothering him.

I look away, watching how the moon hangs high in the inky sky. "So, you're going home?" I try to sound light-hearted, hoping he'll invite me to go along with him, for support, but he doesn't.

"I am home."

"You know what I mean." I finally turn to face him. Even with the stars and the moon, his face is shrouded in shadows. I want to see his eyes, to look deep into them and see his soul. He's clearly hurting, but his admission has nothing to do with it. "Your father is dying."

"Don't you think I know that?" He shoots up, his hands on either side of him, gripping the edge of the mattress. I didn't mean to start a fight, but I need him to see how his handling of this situation is going to live with him forever. Guilt is an emotion that slowly poisons.

"I'm just—"

"Chance, I know what you're doing. And I respect you for pushing me into the direction of wanting me to feel the sadness of saying goodbye to the man who made my life hell, but I can't." His words shock me silent. "This is my life, and you're not a part of it," he bites out, and I know I shouldn't let his anger affect me, but I can't stop it shattering my heart.

"I see." Rising from the bed, I pull on my slacks and shrug on my shirt, knowing I need to get out of here, and I need to do it quickly.

"Wait, I didn't mean—"

"Yes, you did," I interrupt him. Once my shoes are on, I make my way to the nightstand where my phone and wallet are lying along with my car keys.

"I need you in bed with me. Is that so much to ask?" His question jars me, the back and forth emotions are giving me whiplash. I want to be there for him, but how can I when each time I get close enough, he pushes me away?

"Yes. It is. You just told me I'm not a part of your life. I accept your sadness and your heartbreak, but Oliver, I don't accept your anger and rage." I stalk around the bed. Leaning in, I plant a kiss on his scruffy cheek and offer him a smile, even though I know he can't see it. "I would've always been there for you until you chased me away. I didn't expect it to come so soon." My words are merely a whisper, but they're a confession. And I know for a fact he's heard me.

Oliver doesn't look at me. His mouth moves on his own admission. "This is ridiculous. I'm not chasing you out of my house."

"Take care of yourself," I tell him easily, knowing there's not much else to say. We're done. I can't fight a losing battle, and he doesn't have to take every moment to tell me to leave. I'll do him a favor and walk out with my pride intact.

"Chance, get in bed."

"I have to leave," I respond, trying to ease the emotion in my tone.

"Jesus, I don't have the energy for this bullshit, Chance. Just fucking obey me." His roar reverberates throughout the room, and I feel it shaking the walls of his home.

Shaking my head, I speak into the shadows. "You don't own me, Oliver."

He shoves the sheet aside, his feet landing on the floor, and then he's behind me. "I said. Get. In. The. Bed." With every word, he annunciates it with frustration and anger, and that's not the man I love. He's turned into someone I no longer recognize. At this moment, he's not Oliver, not the man who bestowed pleasure on me.

"My father is dying. Do you think—?"

"I'm sorry, Oliver. But like you said, it's your life," I tell him. "There's nothing more I can do for you now." This is the moment I need to decide if I'm willing to play these games or if it is too much. I cast a glance his way, meeting his eyes that are a full-on raging storm. "I can't do this anymore."

"Do what?" he questions, but he knows what I mean. It's there, an unsaid confession of how I feel. He turns his head to look at me. "Don't love me, Chance." His command makes my chest tighten with emotion. Feelings I should've kept to myself, and I realize at this moment, Oliver will never change. He'll never love me, and I make my decision.

Nodding, I turn and walk toward the door. My hand is on the doorknob, but I stop for a moment, inhaling his spicy cologne that hangs heavily in the air. My heart believed what Cayleigh said was right. That Oliver does love me in his own way. Perhaps saying the words would change that. Maybe it will force him to admit how he feels, but it may also push him away. And that's the last thing I want to do. So, instead of voicing my emotions, what's in my heart, I stay silent.

Pondering what he said, I close my eyes and blink away the tears. I've never cried over anyone, never let my pain show, but right now, in the dark, I know I'm safe from him seeing just how he's breaking me.

"You'll be alone forever if you don't let someone in." And with that, I shut the door and make my way to the exit. As soon as I'm out in the fresh night air, I allow the pain to grip me fully, and that's when the tears finally fall. And for the first time in my life, my heart is breaking. Wiping my tears away, I slip into my car and leave the house behind, but I know I'll never leave the man behind because he is ingrained in my heart. He's embedded himself so deep that I know there's no way I'll ever get him out.

He runs within my veins, and he's burrowed right into the very soul of me.

The man is like a goddamn furnace at times, even though his gaze is like an ice-cold snowstorm. Contradictions are part of who he is; a sadist who cares for justice.

A man who can't love, but receives it anyway.

The drive isn't long, and by the time I'm home, I step into the empty apartment, savoring the darkness. I grab a beer from the fridge and settle on the sofa. Flicking on the television, I stare mindlessly at the screen. There's nothing of importance on, but it allows my mind to numb from the thoughts that want to drag me into the depths of my pain.

The silence is gone, and that's what I need. I sip my drink, slowly, as the people on screen talk about sales of products and some other trash as I flick through the channels. I always knew Oliver was angry at life, but this is a newfound rage I saw in him tonight.

And as loudly as I have the sound on the TV, it can't drown out his words.

This is my life, and you're not a part of it.

This is my life, and you're not a part of it.

This is my life, and you're not a part of it.

OLIVER

The coffee drips slowly into the mug as I watch it. Last night, I wanted to admit I loved him, but I couldn't bring myself to say it. As much as I want to say those words, fear holds me back. And in my fear, I pushed him away, more so than I have ever done before.

At first, it didn't bother me, but now as I get ready to drive eight hours north to a small town in Minnesota, I know I made a mistake. This time, I'm not sure it's something I can fix. Shaking my head, I fill the travel mug and screw the lid on tight.

Once everything is packed, I take it out to my SUV, which I hardly ever use. I decided to drive to clear my head, but also, I think deep down, I'm hoping he'll be dead by the time I arrive. Most people would think that's cold-hearted, but I know the truth about who my father is, what he is.

Going home has never been part of my plan. When I walked out, it was forever. When I said goodbye to the man who hurt me more than anyone ever has, I didn't expect to ever look into his steely gray eyes again. I look so much like him, but I'm nothing like the judgmental prick.

Yes, my father is one of those men who has the money, the titles, and you'd think he'd be happy. But he hates everyone who doesn't fit into his perfect mold. Whether it's your race, sexual preference, or even your job, he would sneer, throw insults, and berate you for being who you are.

I lost respect for him a long time ago. And seeing him on his deathbed won't change that, of that I am sure. I lock up the house, slip into the driver's seat, and gun the engine. It's time to go. With one last glance at my phone, I take note that I've only really had four hours of sleep. I laid awake thinking of Chance, wanting to call him to apologize, but like I said, I'm an asshole.

Focusing on the road, I take the highway that leads

toward the I-90, which will take me out of the city. With the buildings whizzing by me, I think back to my father. As much as I hated him, he also made me see what I was doing with my life. He was the one who forced me to wake up from the stupor of pain I'd been living in after the horror I'd faced and move on to better things—more than I'd been doing when I was an immature seventeen-year-old who didn't have any ambition.

"Oliver," his voice rings through the door, and I know he's angry. He's never hit me, never laid a hand on me, but he's emotionally attacked me, and I can always remember the words that have spewed from his mouth. I'm lying on my bed, not wanting to go to school.

Yes, I admit freely how lazy I am. My mother always taught me sloth was the way of the devil—idle hands and all that shit. But I didn't care. I am who I am, and if he can't accept it, too bad. I'll live on my own. My father can pay my way for the rest of my life. It's what he should do after making my childhood shit.

"Oliver, get the fuck out of your bedroom," he growls, banging on my bedroom door like a crazy person. I know why

he's angry. I should've gone to work yesterday. He got me a job down at the local store, but it's not something I want to do.

"I'm busy!"

"Fuck busy, and get your ass out of that godforsaken bedroom, or I'm breaking the door down," he threatens, and I know he'll do it as well. Swiftly, I'm off the bed and pulling open the door before he can bang the fucking thing down. "You're a disgrace. People think there's something wrong with you. Perhaps there is."

"Yes, maybe I'm just not your son. Maybe I have more to give in life than be a fucking emotional punching bag for you." My words are vicious, but that's all he's ever given me. My life has been filled with insults and curse words. I'm seventeen, and I don't need this bullshit.

"Listen to me closely, son,*" he spits the word with venomous intent. "Lazing around all day will never get you out of this one-horse town. Actually, it will ensure you sit here in this dank shithole for the rest of your life." His sneer is cold. His eyes — the same color as mine — shine with rage. And that's when my father utters the words that snap me out of whatever I'd been wallowing in for years. "You'll never make anything of yourself."*

Swinging my bedroom door shut in his face, I turn to my closet. There are clothes strewn everywhere. My floor is littered with takeout containers, dirty underwear, and smoked out joints.

I race to the folding door of my closet, shove it open, and pull out a large backpack, which my dad bought me when I turned sixteen. He was convinced it would allow the traveling bug to hit me. You'd think we were poor the way my bedroom looks, but my father, a lawyer who travels into the city for work almost every day, provides a beautiful house, expensive clothes, and enough food in the kitchen to feed an army.

I've lived with him all my life. My mother died when I was eleven, ensuring I'd never get to see her face age, never be held by her when I was sad, or even hear her voice telling me she loves me. Women are nothing more to me than objects. I'd never loved a woman before, never allowed any of the girls at school near me because I learned early on, they just leave. What's the point in allowing people into your life who aren't going to stick around?

Shoving clothes into my backpack, I ignore my father's muttering from the other side. Even though he's angry and wants me to come out of the room, he'll never walk in. He may threaten me, bang on the door with his fist, but he has never once over the years forced his way in.

Shoving clothes into the bag, I pick up the jeans, T-shirt, and the socks I hid away. I put them at the back of the closet so they'd never see the light of day again. It's been years since I laid eyes on them, and now that I look down at the torn and ripped material, I realize I'm not over what happened.

How can I ever be over it?

A shudder ripples through me when I think about it. The cold fear that seeps into my bones when I recall the night I changed forever is ever-present, and as much as I try to force it down, there's something that still holds me. Memories, images clear as day appear in my mind's eye. Closing my eyes, I think about what happened that night.

"No," I whisper to myself, hoping he doesn't hear me. I can't deal with his cold words right now. I don't want to. Shoving away the image that's fresh in my mind, I force it down as much as I did that night. I push it to the back of my mind, locking it in a box that will never be opened again.

It's time to take charge of my life. Even though I couldn't do it years ago, I'll make something of my life and prove my father wrong. In all my stubbornness, I know I'll be able to look back on this time and be proud of the man I will become.

Once I'm packed, I pull open my bedroom door to meet my father's gaze.

"Where are you going?" He sounds more shocked than I feel. I'm nervous, scared of what I'm about to do, but I know it's the only way.

"I need money. I'm going to Chicago."

He guffaws with malice in the sound. That's one thing I learned about my father. Even when he doesn't want to do it, he's angry and does things out of spite. When I obey him, he sneers; when I don't obey him, he tries to hurt me with words. Either way, he enjoys being an asshole.

"And what are you going to do there?"

"Make something of myself." I shrug, not caring anymore about his snide remarks. "You said I couldn't. I'm going to prove you wrong."

"Oh really?" He crosses his arms in front of his chest. "And you think people are going to want to hire some pansy who can't even clean his room?"

His dig at my sexual orientation isn't new. When he saw me making out with the one boy I thought was cool, he chased him away and insulted me nonstop for months. A hotshot lawyer couldn't be seen with a son who's gay. But what my father doesn't know is I'm bisexual. I found out a long time ago when I kissed Karen Higgins down the road and then came home to jerk off at the memory. And when I kissed Tiago Valera, I did the same thing.

"Fine. I'll pay for you to go into the city, to get into college, but that's it. You're on your own. When you turn twenty-one, I'm done. You'll be your own man," he tells me. That's all I needed him to say. Mainly because I didn't have a cent to my name otherwise, and if there's something my father would love to see, it's his only son fail.

He never once asked why I was so closed off as a teenager. He never once wanted to know who I was as a person. My father was more concerned about his career, about the people who could make him more prominent and ensure he earned more money.

I promised myself when I moved to Chicago I'd never be like him. Slowly, over the years, whenever I felt myself slip into that part of myself, I'd work my way out of the darkness that always engulfed me. And that's where I found my solace in BDSM.

The control allowed me to focus on something outside myself. The memories from my past didn't have a hold over me anymore, and I could be Oliver, the man who built his empire from nothing.

Even though my father paid for my college, once I was done and graduated, I told him to keep his money. I used him as much as he uses people on a daily basis. When I'd first gotten the call that he was sick, I spoke to him. I felt sad that he couldn't tell me himself, but I knew why. When I walked out, I became nothing to him.

My fingers tighten on the steering wheel when I recall that day with such clarity it's as if I'm living in the moment right this minute.

"Dad." My voice is husky with emotion. "They told me. The nurse just hung up. Why didn't you tell me?" As much as I want to hate him, I still feel something for him. That niggling of emotion I long shoved away.

"I'm fine." His anger I'm used to, so his response bitten out is normal to me. "I don't know why you're so bothered. You walked out of the house to live in the big fancy city."

"You paid for me to live here. You told me to leave and make

*something of my life. I did that." I'm angry at his accusation that I wanted to be here. He never showed me an inclination of affection. He never asked me to stay. When I walked out of the house without so much as an "*I'll miss you,*" I knew I'd never be able to walk back into his house without fear of being admonished.*

"You're no son of mine. You're just like your mother, leaving us alone, leaving me alone to live with your shit." That's when it all clicks. He was angry all my life because he saw too much of her in me. The moment I was born, I was hers, not his. And if I didn't look as much like him as I do, I'd wonder if I'm even his son.

"Dad, you know I needed—"

"What? To live in the city so you can fuck any man that comes along? It's disgusting, Oliver. When I wanted a son, I wanted a man, not some fucking pansy."

My blood burns as it thrums through my veins. My hold on the phone is so tight I'm expecting it to shatter in my hand, but it doesn't because I allow myself to feel his anger. My eyes shut tight as I see white sparks behind my lids like a fireworks show.

"You're nothing but a fucking disappointment to me,

Oliver. Fucking around with men is not what God intended for us."

"You're one to talk about what God intended for us. Did Mom know about the whores you were fucking while you were on cases in different cities? No? Well, I did. What do you think that does to a boy?"

"Are you blaming me for your fucking homosexuality?" He's breathing fire through the speaker. I feel it scorch my skin, and I'm certain he'd love to set me alight and watch me burn.

"Why don't you ask Harrison about my homosexuality," I bite out and hang up before he has time to respond. That will leave him with thoughts to linger on. I doubt he'll have the balls to walk up to his brother and ask about me. And that's what I'm banking on.

Shaking my head, I blink a few times and focus on the empty road ahead. My heart gallops at the memory, and I know I'll have to face Harrison again as well. Only this time, I'm all grown up, and I'll make him pay.

Thankfully, Chance isn't here to see me lose it. Because I know the moment I step foot in that house, I'll turn into the monster that sleeps beneath the surface, readying itself for the war that's coming.

OLIVER

Rolling into town, I realize how much hasn't changed. The main road still looks deserted, along with the stores that seem to be on the brink of closure. But it's when I reach the small office where my father would work remotely when he didn't go into the city for a case, that I notice how barren it looks.

Broken Hill is a town time forgot. I never understood why my father lived here, and I doubt I ever will. Exiting the car, I head toward the door, which looks like it's been locked. I recall as a young man, it would always sit partway open as if he were always expecting a rush of clients. But they never came.

This town is where everyone knows your name. They know what you've done and judge you because you're not perfect, much like Mr. Cartwright Michaelson. My knuckles wrap against the glass, and a light flickers on the other side of the window. When the door slides open, I'm met with the old, wrinkled face of Harrison Michaelson. My grandparents must've hated my dad and his brother.

Both sons were vile monsters. Perhaps not of the same caliber. My father wasn't sick like my uncle was, but deep down, if push came to shove, I have a feeling good old Cartwright wouldn't think twice about taking what didn't belong to him.

God knows, he probably has done already. I've only been blind to it because I never wanted to be near him. The farther I was from daddy dearest, the happier I was.

I can't believe I was born into a family so fragmented by darkness and filth. It's as if their minds had broken, shattered, and nothing was allowed in unless it was immoral and vile.

"Oliver." He seems shocked to see me. Perhaps he thought I wouldn't return. Maybe he's scared I returned to tell everyone about his dark secret he's hidden away for so long.

"I'm here to sign off on my father's will and sell the house." I don't bother greeting him. He doesn't deserve it nor has ever earned my respect. There's nothing this man can say to me which will make me feel sorry for him.

He steps aside, allowing me into the small space. The once beautifully furnished office is a wasteland of broken chairs and papers strewn on every available surface.

"You're handling the paperwork?" I arch a brow at him as he makes his way back behind the desk. His body is slightly hunched over, and his fingers bent and crooked from arthritis. He looks like shit.

"Your father wanted me to finalize everything before you arrived. Granted, he didn't think you'd come and told me to courier documents to you once he signed them." He speaks, but he doesn't look me in the eye.

The air thickens with anger, which emanates from me. I want to rage at him, shout, scream, something, but I hold onto my restraint, which is tugged taut. The fine line close to snapping, along with all my control.

This man before me is old and withered, not the

person I recall from years ago when he sat back and watched the pain I endured. He enjoyed it. There was satisfaction in his eyes that ripped through me so deep it tore right through my soul.

Perhaps that explains why I'm so fucked up. Maybe that's the reason I enjoy doling out pain, watching my submissives take what I give and smiling when they whimper and beg me for more. The only difference is, I don't force the agony on them, not like the man before me allowed it to happen.

He finally shoves the pages into a folder, shuts it, and I watch his wrinkled hand as it rests on the cover. I voice the question that's been on the tip of my tongue for months, years, and even right now. I don't know if I should ask it. Because, if he gives me the answer I'm expecting, I may kill him with my bare hands.

But I ask it anyway. "Does he know?" I question, waiting for him to nod, but he doesn't. Of course, both assholes never confessed anything to each other. "You've never told your brother what you did to me?"

The man can't look me in the eye. Guilt slumps his shoulders, and his hands tremble and shake. I'm proud of myself for being strong enough to face him. He knows what he did, along with his friend, or should I say, life partner. They forced me into doing something so vile and despicable. He watched me break, and, he didn't lift a goddamn finger to help.

"You're as fucked up as my father."

"Don't speak ill of the dying," he bites out, finally looking at me. His one eye is blueish gray, and I wonder if it has anything to do with a cataract that now blinds him. I don't ask, as I don't care.

"I want to get this done as soon as possible."

"Are you going to see him?" he asks, his brows lifting in question, and I wonder if it's time to go to my father and tell him just why I walked out. Perhaps it's time he learned the truth of what happened so many years ago.

"Maybe. Get the paperwork done. I'll come back tomorrow." Turning on my heel, I head for the door. I hear the shuffling of papers as I tug the handle, allowing fresh air to fill my lungs.

"Oliver," he calls to me. I stop, but I don't face him. "I'm sorry."

Shrugging off his apology, I step outside and shut the door behind me with a loud bang, almost shattering the window pane. I've always wanted some form of recognition that he knew what he did was wrong, but he never gave it to me. Instead, he acted as nothing had happened. And that's what hurt the most.

But I've overcome that. It's no longer something that bothers me. Instead, I've grown from the experience and become a better man than either of the men who should've been role models for me.

Pulling out my phone, I tap out a message to Chance.

Oliver: ***I'm sorry.***

It's all I can offer him for now. I care about him, but I can't give him the words he craves. I can't tell anyone how I feel until I finally lay my father to rest. I realize I needed this. To come back to the place that broke me and burn it to the ground.

Slipping into the driver's seat, I turn the engine and pull out onto the road. There's a small hotel on the outskirts of town where I've booked a room for two nights. I don't need to be here for longer than that. The sooner I can get home, the better.

And the sooner I can talk to Chance and make him see how this wasn't my fault, or his. This was because of a man I trusted, a man who turned my genuine love into a filthy emotion.

Each person in my life I was meant to love or was responsible for teaching me about love, broke me. They took all I had to give, and I was left empty. A vacant shell. Even my father, who would never believe the pain I'd endured and couldn't offer me solace in a world he was meant to keep me safe from.

Growing up with people judging your every move, your every choice, it breaks a child. It rips you to pieces, and you're left with nothing more than a frail heart that can no longer hold emotion.

From my father, I learned the more women you fuck, the happier you are. But I realized early on it wasn't true. He may have seemed happy, but there wasn't a light in his eyes. His smile was sour, filled with regret and guilt.

My mother died when I was far too young to know her properly, and I never got a chance to know what that kind of affection is like. So, I focused on fucking. I focused on the need to dominate and control. Instead of wanting a woman to hold me, I craved and hungered to make them cry and scream.

Watching beautiful porcelain flesh mar with red welts is one of the most beautiful things a man like me can experience. My mind is running one hundred miles a minute as I shake away the thoughts.

Being back in this town has dredged up ghosts from the past, and I'm here to lay them all to rest beside my father. There's no longer a reason for me ever to come back here. Once he's buried, I will turn my back on this town and only look forward.

When I pull up to the hotel and exit the car, I glance at my phone — no response. I know he's angry. He has every right to be. Perhaps I should call him. Stepping into the hotel lobby, I find a woman I don't recognize at the desk.

"Good evening." She smiles, still sleepy from her droopy eyes.

"Oliver Michaelson. I booked a room."

She glances at the book on the desk in front of her,

then nods. "Yes," she tells me while handing me a set of keys. Two gold, slim-cut keys, which I know one is for the room, the other for the front door the guests use if they're out in the evening.

"Thank you." I don't wait for her to tell me about the rules. I won't be here for that long. Making my way up to the second floor, I unlock the door and head into the small space which has one double bed, a wardrobe against the opposite wall, and a window overlooking the forest beyond.

Memories seep through my mind, attacking me violently when I see the trees where I used to hide from the monsters. When I was a child, it was the most magical place in the world. But the older I got, I realized monsters didn't hide under the bed at night like we were all led to believe. They hid in plain sight.

They were people you loved and trusted.

People who told you fairy tales. And scary stories.

They were the people who said they care, told they loved you, but it wasn't with sweet affection. No. It was with a violence that would shatter your world.

I leave my suitcase on the bed, then pick up my

cell phone. No response. I'd thought he would at least give me a chance to explain my anger and rage, or even attempt to apologize, but the reality is, I don't deserve it. I always knew I wasn't worthy of Chance Moore. And it hits me right in the gut — I don't deserve *him*.

Chance is a good man. He loves with everything he has, just like his sister. When I think about Peyton, I wonder then if she may know where he may be. They're close, and I'm positive if he were to confess anything to someone, it would be her.

Glancing at my phone, I decide I may as well give her a call. I want to talk to him. I need to find some way of apologizing to him for my anger. I scroll through my contact list and find Peyton's number before I have time to rethink my actions.

She may not want to tell me where he is. If she knows what an asshole I've been, she may tell me to leave her brother alone, but there is a possibility she'll understand and want to help me.

I've never felt so unworthy of someone before. Yes, my demons want to darken Chance's light. They want to play with him until there's nothing left, but I won't let that happen. This is the one chance I have to make things right.

So, I hit dial on the number and press the phone to my ear. Waiting for her to answer has me holding my breath. Tension tightens my shoulders, and my heart is thudding in my throat. I feel like a goddamn teenager.

"Hello, Oliver," she says into the speaker, but her tone is serious, far too serious, and I realize he's probably told her. I don't blame him. If I were in his shoes, I would've done the same.

"Peyton, do you know where your brother—?"

"You know what, Oliver," she starts, interrupting me. "There are many things I can accept from people. I mean, Carrick broke my heart, but he realized being an asshole wasn't going to win him any points. I'm—"

"Look, Peyton—"

"I'm not done. Either you listen to me, or I hang up on you."

I don't know how Carrick handles her, but deep down, I know she's right. "Fine."

"My brother doesn't go around fucking random people because it's fun. He has wanted to be with you for as long as he's been in Chicago, and when you finally allowed him in, you push him away. Playing with his feelings, toying with him like he means nothing to you is not something that will earn my respect," she admonishes me like I'm one of the girls. "Now, either you sort your shit out wherever you are and come home and fight for him, or you stay there, and leave my brother to find someone who loves him for who he is."

He hasn't told her why I'm here. My heart fills with a foreign feeling that leaves me breathless. Even though I hurt him brutally with my words, he's not given away any of my secrets. He's not even told his sister why I'm here, and that means more to me than any four-letter word that could ever be uttered.

"I'll fight for him, Peyton."

"Can you love him the way he deserves to be loved?" she questions, stilling me for a moment. She's waiting for me to admit it. To tell her that even though I've never been so scared of opening myself up before, I've already done it without noticing. Chance has made me love even when I was convinced I couldn't.

"Yes." The word rings true. It vibrates through me,

and I allow myself to taste it on my tongue for a moment before I finally confess to her. "I love him, Peyton."

"Don't tell me." She smiles; I can hear it in her words. "He's the one who needs to hear it. But there's one thing I will tell you, Oliver Michaelson. If you ever hurt Chance, I'll rip your heart out with my bare hands."

This causes me to chuckle. The small minx is feisty. There's a fire that burns inside her, and I can see why Carrick loves her so much. She's not just a submissive, she's a confident, independent woman, and that's more alluring than any whore, any woman who throws themselves at you.

"I don't doubt that, Peyton. I don't doubt that at all. Thank you for being the one to set me straight this time," I tell her. It's true. I recall the day I had to talk her off the ledge, and I suppose karma is coming back around, and she's given me a payoff I don't believe I deserve.

"Friendship and family are more than just blood, Oliver. They're who has your best interests at heart. My brother and I were lucky enough to find our family here in Chicago."

"You're rather wise, young lady."

"I learned from the best," she tells me, and I know she's referring to the talk we had a long while ago. When I helped her with Carrick, I offered her a long talk about emotions, family, and letting someone in. I feel like a hypocrite at times, but seeing my friends and those I consider family happy, it makes me feel like I've helped.

"Is Chance—?"

"He's not here, but I'm guessing he's at home, probably wallowing in a damn bottle of Scotch or something." Her voice has a lightness to is, but I can hear the frustration in the undertone. I've caused that, and it hurts me.

"Peyton, I'm learning," I tell her. "This, your brother, it's all caught me in a whirlwind I never expected."

"Oh, I know that, Mr. Michaelson," she tells me, and this time, I know she's smiling for real. "Just remember what you told me — it's time to let someone learn about who you are, and for you to learn about them.

"If you give him a call, he'll probably ignore you. My brother is one of those people who will let you stew for a little while before he lets you back in," Peyton tells me before a screech of a little voice comes from her side of the line. "Shit. I have to go," she tells me, causing me to chuckle.

"Thank you, sweetheart. Take care of the girls, and make sure to give Rick my best," I tell her.

"I will. Thank you, Oliver. Just look after my brother. Take care. And come home soon." Once she hangs up, I realize what she said. *Come home soon.*

"I will."

CHANCE

The sun is setting on the horizon, and the two words Oliver messaged me are lingering at the back of my mind. They haunt me, but as much as I want to respond, I don't. He needs to realize when you hurt someone, it's not as easy as saying I'm sorry, and those two words don't make everything right.

Shutting my phone off, I focus on the screen before me. I'd been working on a business plan after talking to Carrick earlier. I want to open another club like Nathan's done in LA, and he's offered to look through the plan I have.

It's a lot of work, but I'm hoping my focus can be put to better use than the downward spiral I'd been on before I came to Chicago. Even when Peyton left to come and see Savvie a couple of years ago, I knew I wouldn't be able to continue on the path I'd taken.

I need to stop sitting around waiting for opportunities to fall into my lap. My first step toward that was signing Oliver's contract, but now it's time to take my professional life and create a career I'm proud of.

The doorbell rings, dragging my concentration away from the computer. Rising from my seat, I head to the door and pull it open.

"Chance, good to see you." Nathan smiles. He's looking good with his dark hair tousled, his eyes dark and broody, and his smooth, sharp features, giving him a European look.

"Thanks for meeting with me, Nate." I step aside, allowing him into the apartment. When I invited him to give me some pointers on the business, he gladly accepted. He'd been in town to see Rick and Mason, and I figured I'd take the opportunity to talk to him directly rather than on a call.

"I'm always happy to help entrepreneurs," he offers, settling into the seat I gesture toward. "And this has been a great investment for me. Sins of Seven Los Angeles has seen substantial growth in clients over the past six months. Once we vetted the scum, we found a number of people who need the club."

"I think having a safe place to learn, practice, and meet others in the lifestyle is important. Honestly, I didn't think about this until I had some time last night."

"Where's Oliver?"

I knew he'd ask. I didn't expect the mention of the man's name to affect me so much, but my chest tightens at the thought of him not being here, or me not being with him through this difficult time.

"He had family business to deal with," I respond, waving it off as if it's nothing. But when I meet Nathan's dark gaze, I know he knows what's going on. His expression tells a thousand words.

"Is it his father?" he asks, and I wonder how much to divulge. This isn't my story to tell, and offering up Oliver's secrets is not up to me. "He came here when he was just seventeen because of the old man. His father is a piece of work."

"You know him?"

"Not personally. I grew up in much the same environment as Oliver did. Rich family, beautiful mansions, expensive cars, but when my mother found out about my *needs,* she wanted nothing more than to disown me, but she had to keep up appearances."

"Fuck, I'm so sorry."

Nate shrugs. "I confessed my life story one night to Oliver when we were at college together. I told him why I have this innate need to humiliate and degrade women. And he realized we had so much more in common than we'd anticipated."

Flicking the pen between my fingers, I want to ask, but I'm afraid to learn more about Oliver. What if it's something I can't look past or something that will change the way I feel about him?

"He's closed himself off to everything. I've tried. I can't do it," I admit, shaking my head when I recall the words he uttered to me.

"Listen to me," Nate says. "I was like Oliver, so much so that I craved seeing my submissives broken to the point of them wanting to run away. I wanted them to hate me because I hated me. I never let myself forgive those in my past, and that's what broke me."

"What do you mean?"

"When I was fifteen, I was attacked by a group of men and women," he tells me, his voice cracking along with my heart. "I'd been forced to do things . . ." When Nate shakes his head, I know this is no joke. It's torn him into pieces, and I realize we have so much more in common than I could've imagined.

"I . . ." My words fall into silence when I try to figure out how to say this. "I know how it feels; only, I was paid to be at a party a long while ago. The man I was dating, the man I thought I could trust, he . . ." My eyes burn, and my body shudders when I recall the memories of that night.

It's been so long since I allowed myself to go back there. And now that I've done it twice in the last week, I find myself slipping.

"Hey." Nathan's voice is hard, commanding, causing me to look up at him. "You're stronger than your past. Anyone who can survive something like that and function on the other side of it is brave and resilient."

"Four men. And me. And I didn't know how I

would ever survive."

"But you did," he insists again. He doesn't reach for me, and I'm grateful. I'm not sure I would be as calm thinking about it with someone touching me. "Have you told Oliver?"

I nod.

"Then let him finish what he needs to, but don't hate him before you learn about his past. There's so much more to him than you think. Yes, he's a cold, calculated bastard at times, but he can love. Just let him."

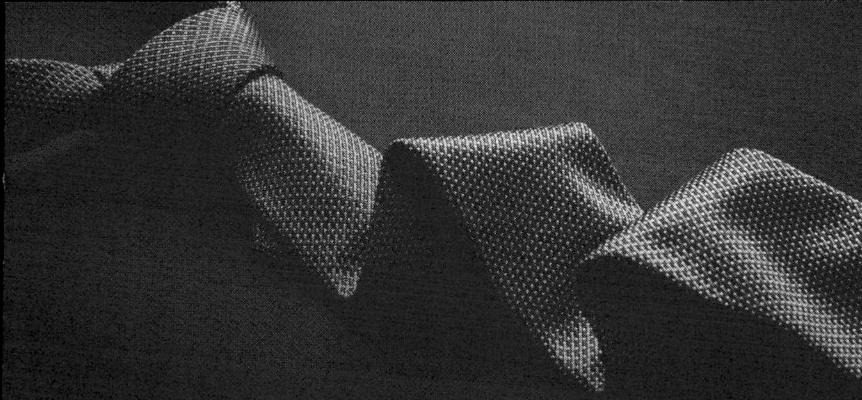

OLIVER

Staring up at the ceiling, I focus on the patterns, wondering how much more I can fuck up this thing between Chance and me. Yes, I told him I can't offer him a forever, a relationship, but what I said, and how I said it, that was uncalled for. And of course, I only realized when it was too late.

The thoughts of Chance meld with the images of standing at my father's grave, and finally laying the old bastard to rest. I want Chance beside me, he should be there, but I can't explain my feelings for him. I've never admitted to myself, or anyone else in my life that I loved them, but perhaps now, with Chance, I can finally allow myself to let someone in.

The memory of my father's anger at finding Tiago

and me flits through my mind, reminding me of how he reacted when he learned about me and my feelings for Tiago.

"Oliver, you know the kids in school are never going to understand how we feel," he pleads with me. Tiago's big brown eyes stare right through me. I know he's right. They'll bully us until we graduate and leave this shithole town behind.

The city would've been so much easier. I hate my father in that moment for forcing us to live here. I've always wanted to live in a big city where nobody knows who I am, or what I am. It's difficult enough pleasing my father, making sure I'm the perfect son to follow in his footsteps but to parade around school and act like those jocks, that's not who I am.

Nodding, I turn away from the boy who's caught my eye. The first boy to ever reciprocate my feelings. "I know," I answer him, but I can't face him. My chest aches; my heart is thrumming against my ribs. I've never been more nervous before, because when I turn to him, I see his smile.

Deep dimples dip into his cheeks. They're cute, sexy even, and I watch his full lips tilt up into a shy smile. I've always known I was different. And I'm okay with that. It's everyone else that worries me.

"Come here, Oliver," he says in that accent, a gentle lilt of Spanish. He moves closer toward me, his one hand holding my cheek. Even though he's taking the lead, I don't allow him that position for too long, because soon, my hand is tangled in his black curls as I tug him closer.

Our lips mold together. The gentleness of his kiss is foreign, but it feels so right. However, the second it's there, the next moment, it's gone. And as soon as I open my eyes, I find the angry, steel gray of my father's glare.

"What the fuck is going on here?" Cartwright Michaelson, my father, is like a raging tornado that sweeps through you without you knowing what happened. His voice booms across the garden, and I'm stumbling backward in an attempt to stay out of the eye of the storm.

Tiago is on the ground, his ass hitting the grass with a loud thud, and then my father is rounding on me. Storming toward me like a fucking hurricane, he raises his hand but stills the moment he realizes what he's doing. It's the first and only time he's attempted to hit me.

"Get the fuck inside and wait in the kitchen."

"But, Dad—"

He pins me with a stare so fierce I shut my mouth and head inside with one lingering glance at Tiago, and I know it's the last time I'll ever see the boy with the big brown eyes and shaggy black hair.

I wonder just how I'm meant to look my father in the eyes and tell him everything I'd wanted to say for most of my life. Yes, there are things he probably knows already, like how much I hate him, but to admit I broke because of something I should've been able to control, that's what scares me the most.

Picking up my phone, I scroll through the list of recent calls and find the one that glares at me accusingly. I know I shouldn't call because of how I left things, but he's the only person who can calm me down right now. At least, get me into the right headspace for this shit show.

Since he walked out of my house last night, I vowed not to bend and break by contacting him, but I can't help myself. Pressing the phone to my ear, I listen to the ringing, silently pleading for him to pick up the phone, for him to hear me out, and perhaps agree to come here and see me face to face so we can sort out the tension and anger between us.

"Oliver." My name is uttered with wariness, causing me to shut my eyes in frustration. I did this to us. He was ready to love me, and I practically told him he meant nothing to me.

"I needed to know you're okay."

Silence greets me. But I can hear his breathing. He's sitting there, listening to my short, nervous breaths, and I wonder what he's thinking. He doesn't say anything for a long while, but then he awards me with a response.

"I'm fine." Two of the scariest words I'll ever hear in my life. Love is a strange emotion. It takes hold of you, holding you safe in its warmth, but when it's hurt or broken, it burns you from the inside out.

"I should be home in the next couple of days," I tell him.

He sighs. "Okay. Well, I'm busy at the moment. Is there something you wanted?"

Is there?

I don't know.

"Yes. I'd like a meeting in my office on Friday

morning. We'll cancel whatever time is left on the contract and bring this arrangement to an end."

He doesn't breathe for long moments. There's nothing on the other end, just silence that deafens me. I wait for him to refuse my offer. To tell me he wants me, for me to see how much he cares. And at this moment, I want him to say the words. To admit he loves me.

"Fine. See you Friday."

The tone in his voice, the finality of what's coming only seems to make my chest hurt, and my lungs struggle to pull in air. In all the years of training submissives, I've never once wanted one of them to stick around. Even when I canceled an agreement early, I was always happy to see them go off and be happy. But all I can think of is the pain in my chest.

Swinging my legs over the edge of the bed, I shrug on my shirt and pull up the slacks I'd discarded earlier. With my jacket on, I forgo the tie and grab the keys to my car. It's time to face the man who I used to call a father. Outside, I take a long deep breath, attempting to focus on the task at hand, but there's nothing that can take away the words Chance just uttered.

Regret — a motherfucker punch to the gut.

Driving down roads that bring back memories, I turn into the driveway of the two-story home I grew up in. Everything about it is the same, except it's aged along with my father. It's no longer shiny and new. There's paint peeling, the windows are cracked, and the wood is slowly rotting.

Seeing it in this state only confirms what I always knew. When everything seems picturesque and serene on the outside, don't be fooled by it. Beneath that shiny exterior can be a dark, ugly rot infesting in every crevice. And slowly but surely it will seep through, and soon, you're as ugly as you are on the inside. People will soon see you for what you truly are.

I shove the door open and exit the car. I hear the creak of the door before I see him. When my father steps out onto the porch, I don't recognize him at first. He's no longer the strong, formidable man I once knew.

The frailty of his frame is evident. The sickness has eaten away at him, and the clothes he once held so dear to him are torn and ratty. He doesn't look like an infamous lawyer anymore. No, my father looks like a homeless person.

"Oliver?"

I step closer to the house, needing to see him close up. The moment I do, I see myself, and the image cuts through me like a sleek, hot blade through butter. This could be me in twenty odd years, and it scares the shit out of me.

He's tortured. His face holds wrinkles that are worn in from the lies and guilt. His gaze is ice, pain, and regret shining in them as he watches me. Chance's words burn me at that moment.

If you don't let someone in, you'll die alone.

Alone.

Dying.

He croaks out the words, "You came."

"I had to sort out the paperwork," I tell him as I step up onto the porch. Family reunions are meant to be emotional exchanges — hugs and kind words — but this is nothing like that.

I watch my father nod, then gesture for me to enter the house. As soon as I do, I'm hit by the agony of a seventeen-year-old boy. I'm hit so harshly by the memory of hobbling home that day that tears burn my eyes.

It was the last day I ever cried. And even now, I don't allow myself to let it happen. Instead, I blink back the tears and take in the house.

"Did you want something to drink?" My father raises his brows in what? Hope?

Nodding, I offer him a response. "Sure. Whiskey if you have it."

He turns and heads down the hallway toward our kitchen, and I make my way to the patio door. The garden that was once lush and manicured looks like an overgrown forest. Weeds are taking over, and the grass that was once bright green is now a dreary yellow — dried out and dying, just like Cartwright Michaelson.

"Here you go." My father enters the room, handing me a glass, then settling in his recliner. The old piece of furniture has been his favorite for so long, and if I ever attempted to perch my ass in it, he'd practically drag me from the chair and dump me on the sofa. "I didn't think you'd come." His voice is pained, and the tension in the room is thick and heavy, like a fog rolling in.

Watching him for a moment, I notice how his body slumps against the left arm of the chair. He looks like he's not going to move for days, and I wonder if that will be the spot where he'll take his last breath.

The morbid thoughts grip me in their feral hold. Reminding me of just how much time I've been away. When I last saw my father, he was strong, tall, with broad shoulders, and his head was thick with salt-and-pepper hair.

Now though, he's almost bald, his skin is shallow, and the way it hangs from his bones makes me think he could easily break. Old age, sickness, it takes its toll, and perhaps it was my father's lifestyle of drinking and whores that made him ill. Maybe it was the way karma turned around to bite him in the ass, but he looks nothing like the Cartwright Michaelson I used to call dad.

"Well, I'm the only offspring. They called me. You didn't tell me your brother is working for you." It's a statement, an angry one, but he merely waves my comment off.

"All these years, you've never told me why you're so angry at him. He's your unc—"

"He's no fucking family of mine!" I bite out, rearing my hand back, flinging the tumbler against the far wall, causing my father to cringe in shock.

"Are you going to tell a dying man why?" he questions, lifting his dreary gaze to mine. I settle on the sofa and watch him for a moment, contemplating his request. Do I tell my father what happened to me, or do I allow him to die in peace?

CHANCE

Hitting send on the email, I sit back, happy with the work I've put into the business plan. As much as I focused on what I needed to do, Oliver's request is still replaying in my mind on a never-ending loop.

If he wants to cancel the agreement, it means he wants to move on. At least, that's what it seems like. I rise, heading into the living room, and I flop onto my sofa, closing my eyes. I want to call him. My fingers itch to talk, to hit dial on his number, or tap out a message to him, but I have to allow him to make the first move.

"Damn you, Oliver Michaelson," I tell the empty room. My phone buzzes wildly then, vibrating on the countertop in the kitchen. As soon as I reach the object, the ringing stops, and restarts. The screen lights up with

Oliver's name, and I contemplate not answering. But he wouldn't call again if it wasn't urgent.

"Oliver."

"Chance, forgive me."

My brows furrow. It's almost midnight, and I wonder if he's drunk. "What?"

I'm met with silence, and I wonder if he hung up after dialing me, realizing it was a bad idea. "I saw my father today." His words are filled with pain so acute I feel it over the line right to the core of me.

"Okay. But why are you calling me, Oliver? I told you, I can't do this. Your back and forth is—"

"Chance, I want you here." His words come out in a loud whoosh. They tumble over the line, leaving me confused.

"You want me. You don't want me. Oliver, I'm not a toy. I'm not yours to own," I tell him. "I love you. If that's too much for you to handle, then we end this right here. I can't *not* love you." A weight is lifted from my shoulders as I confess my feelings. The words I'd been holding in for so long finally tumble free, and I feel like a man who's finally taking control.

"I know. I'm a mess. I've always been a mess. Even though it seems as if I'm in control, my personal life is far from it. Chance, I don't know how to deal with this anymore."

I have a feeling this is the most challenging thing he's ever had to do. The trepidation in his voice is evident. He's nervous. I doubt Oliver has ever had to give up his control, and perhaps that's where the story lies.

Losing control.

"Come to me. I'll send a driver to collect you and drive you up here. Or if you want to fly, then I'll have my private plane fly you here." He finally breathes over the line.

"But I don't understand why. I mean, you wanted to end our contract." I settle on the stool because my legs are shaking, my hands are trembling, and I'm losing all my confidence. I want him, and I need him to say these things, but what if he changes his mind tomorrow? Fear trickles down my spine at the thought.

"I've never been a man to beg. I've always had others pleading with me, but right now, I am begging you, Chance. You've broken me down. I need you here.

Please." His voice cracks on the word. I wonder if he's ever needed to say it to anyone before. I doubt it. He's never been in a relationship, if that's even what we have. "If you come up to see where my past lies, I'll give you everything, Chance. I promise."

When he goes silent, I know he's leaving this up to me. He's not ordering me. He's not commanding me.

"Fine, get the plane ready. I'll be at the airport in an hour."

His breathing leaves his mouth in a relieved sigh, and I know I've just made the right choice. I don't know what happened between him and his father, but it must've made him realize he's losing me.

"I will. See you soon." He hangs up before I can respond, and I know there's no turning back. If this is going to work, I need to walk in there with my guard up. I can't be hurt again, and I can't take his bullshit anymore.

I'm coming Oliver, and this time, you're going to give me what I need, or it's over.

As soon as the plane touches down and we're on the tarmac, I see him. From the small window of the plane, I notice Oliver standing under a lamp post near his car. As always, he's dressed in a suit, nothing out of place.

Moments later, I've disembarked, and we're standing opposite each other. Neither of us making a move to say anything. He offers a nod after a while, then gestures for the car.

"Let's get to the hotel," he utters, not greeting me, not telling me anything other than that. I'm not sure what to make of him, of his actions, but I slip into the passenger seat of his SUV and focus on the road ahead.

With quick glances at his hands, I notice how they're gripping the steering wheel with white-knuckle ferocity. It's not far, and soon we're pulling into a parking lot with a couple of cars on the far end. This place really is the ass-end of nowhere. I can't believe a man like him grew up in a small town like this.

The contrast is alarming. He's made so much of his life, and clearly, from so much of nothing. And I know there's a story in there somewhere. There must be. We exit the car wordlessly, Oliver's cool exterior once again in place. The man from the phone call hours ago is no longer here, and instead, I'm met with the Dominant.

"Thanks for coming," he says when we step into the room. The place is small compared to his house, and the size is stifling when we're both inside. I turn to him, meeting those gray eyes that hold all the secrets he knows he'll need to divulge soon enough.

"Why am I here, Oliver?" I finally voice the question that's been sitting on my tongue for the past however many hours. I'm tired, I'm frustrated, and I'm unsure what he wants from me. On the phone, he said one thing, and now that I'm standing in front of him, he's acting aloof, as if my presence is no longer needed.

"You asked me to show you who I am," he says, his voice distant, as if he's unsure of showing me the man who's hidden beneath so many layers of hurt and pain. He's at the window, and I watch as he blocks out most of the view, but I can see the forest beyond—nothing there besides the dark trees.

"Yes, and you told me I'm not a part of your life. Then you left, and I had to figure out what to do. Now you've got me here. It's time for you to either tell me your story or let me go." I'm not sure where my strength comes from, the courage to voice the words I should've said in his house two nights ago. "When I walked out, I meant it. I won't be a toy for you. I won't be something you can push and pull at your will."

"I know." He nods. "It's not fair of me to expect you to stay when you don't understand. So, I figured, the best way for you to understand is to listen to what happened."

"Okay," I respond. Sitting on the mattress, I watch him for a moment. For the first time since I met him, Oliver is visibly nervous. His expression may be stoic, but it's the tension rolling off him that gives him away.

He sighs, then begins to speak. "I was fifteen when I found out I was bisexual." His words are drenched in sadness, which grips my heart, holding on for dear life. "It was eye-opening. All the boys at school were looking at porn on their phones. They would whisper and chuckle about breasts and pussy. At a glance, I was just like them. Looking at a naked woman made my cock hard."

He smiles, shaking his head as he sips his coffee before he settles on the stool at the breakfast bar. He doesn't say anything for a while, and I know I can't interrupt him. I need to know who Oliver is, and if he doesn't open up to me, I'm not sure I can stay.

"When I first kissed a girl, it was like fireworks shooting through me. We'd gotten to second base, and I was proud of myself, but," He sighs, his stare finding mine. "There was also a boy I'd had strange feelings for. I was confused for a long time before he finally made a move."

Shaking his head, he spins the mug on the counter. The sound is the only thing I hear apart from my heart, which seems to be racing wildly in my chest.

"He kissed me in my backyard, but my father caught us. However, it was the single most erotic thing I'd ever felt. He groped my cock, and even though I was confused as hell, I wanted more. I wanted both him and the girl together, in my room and naked."

"And I'm guessing your father didn't approve?"

He shakes his head. "No, not by a long shot. He dragged me inside and gave me a tongue lashing I'd never forget. One thing about Cartwright Michaelson, he never hit me. Physically, he left me alone, but emotionally, he basked in making me hurt in ways no strike could ever touch."

My legs feel shaky. My chest is pained, my heart cracking with his admission. I had a family who accepted me for who I was. They never once admonished me for what I wanted or who I wanted. They supported me no matter what, and to hear someone else was insulted because he desired something different makes me sick.

"For a long time, I tampered down my feelings. But it got out. Someone saw the kiss I'd had with Tiago," he tells me sadly, and my gut lurches. "It was the moment my life would be changed forever."

I'm not sure what it is, but an acute pain in my chest from Oliver's tone of voice stills my breathing for a moment. I can't explain it, but I've never felt more connected to someone in my life, and now that he's finally allowing me in, letting me see the most broken part of him, I want to confess my feelings. I want to tell him I love him while looking into his eyes. I want him to see the truth, but when I open my mouth, and before

I can, he continues.

"One day, three guys from school caught me walking home," he utters. "I was a scrawny kid. They were a year older, bullies. I normally kept my head down, but they seemed to want to target me that day."

He sighs, the sound like a foghorn in the moon hanging in the dark sky, the silver streaming through the window. It's strange when someone confesses their innermost fears. It tears you apart as the observing party. And there's nothing you can do to ease the pain of memories.

"They dragged me off into the edge of the park where it met the forest not far from my house. Kicking, spitting on me, they went to town. One eye swelled up. I could just about see them. Then I heard a booming voice, deep and commanding. It was as if an angel had been sent to save me."

Glancing away, I close my eyes and breathed deeply, calming myself at the thought of a young boy, scared, alone, and hurt — all because he wanted to love.

"He picked me up after chasing the bullies away. Took me into his home to patch me up. I thanked him."

There's a wry smile on his face, but the despondency in his expression tells me there's so much more to his story.

"Oliver—"

"He chuckled, told me boys will be boys, but he can help me."

"That's good," I offer, leaning forward, praying with everything I have that he was going to be okay after that. Wishing this person was good. But Oliver shatters everything when he finally continues.

"He pulled me from the chair once I was all cleaned up and shoved me over the table. He ripped my pants down and told me he'd show me what it's like to be gay. His body loomed over mine. He forced himself deep inside me, and he clamped his hand over my mouth to keep any screams from alerting passersby."

Tears prick my eyes, and Oliver turns blurry in my eye line. The lump in my throat widens, thickens painfully. I want to say something, but I can't find the words. There's nothing I can say. Blinking, I allow my emotions to drip down my cheeks. I want to reach out to him, to hold him, to make him see I love him, but I don't. Fear holds me back.

"When he was done, he shoved me out the door, and I practically crawled home. When I got there, I showered and spent most of my time in bed. Over the next two years, I became a recluse. My father thought I was just lazy, but I was broken."

"I'm so . . . Fuck, Oliver," I mumble, my voice is low, a whisper, but he hears me.

He lifts his eyes to find mine staring back at him. "When I finally turned seventeen, I knew I needed to get out of there. I had one more year of school, but I couldn't do it. So, my father paid for me to come to the city and finish up there. I decided from that day on I'd never allow anyone to take away my control."

"You never told your father?"

He shakes his head. "Even if I did, he would've laughed and told me it's because I was gay. He didn't believe in bisexuality. He didn't even believe that two women could love each other. My father grew up as a good Catholic boy."

He sighs so loudly the pain etched in the sound only makes my chest tighten, my heart ached, and my throat thickens with a lump of emotion that's threatening to choke me.

"The problem is there was one witness to what happened to me. A man I trusted with all my heart, and he broke every ounce of that trust."

"What? Who?"

"My uncle. You see, my uncle is gay, but he's hidden it from my father, his brother, all their lives. He knows what my father is like, so he's lived in secret with the man who violated me. George Welham was a vile man. He had been married before and had a daughter. One day, I'd gone to his house to pick up school work since I was in the same grade as Nikita, and…"

The words taper off into nothing, and my body is tense when he meets my gaze once more. Guilt burns in those dark orbs and I realize with sickening clarity what had happened.

"They forced me to do something to attempt to *fix* me. The physical pain for me and her may have eased up, perhaps even healed and we could have moved on with our lives. But what broke me was the emotional agony."

"Jesus, that's so fucked up, Oliver. You needed

support, not judgment." I can't take it anymore and make my way toward him. He doesn't push me away when I close the distance between us. Reaching for his face, I take in the fine lines that crease at the corners of his eyes, the dusting of salt and pepper on his sharp jawline, and the way his eyes shimmer with hidden emotion.

"That's who I am, Chance. The ugly, sordid story of how I became what I am. I enjoy doling out pain because I want to feel release. It now offers me pleasure. When I arrived in Chicago, I met a Dominant, a sadist, and he taught me to be what I am. He showed me there's another way to deal with the anger."

"And you spent that time learning." It's not a question, but he nods anyway.

"I was young, at college, met Nathan, and when he'd confessed what he had been through, I knew we would be friends forever. He was my best friend, still is, and alongside him, we found closure in our agony."

He turns away, and I don't feel angry, just sad that he has to deal with the memories that seem to be as volatile as the ones I deal with daily. He stares out the window, and I can't help but take him in. If something like that had happened to anyone else, they'd be broken. I may have been hurt, but it wasn't family who did it. I could walk away from the strangers and never see them again.

But for Oliver, he had to spend every day looking at the man he trusted. A man who not only broke that trust but also broke him emotionally. I step closer to his frame, but I don't touch him, but I stand behind him.

We're silent, but he knows what it means. I'm here for him. And I finally know he wants me here. I don't ask about his father. I allow him time to work through the feelings I'm sure are currently waging war through his mind.

I know we'll get through this.

I know it right down to my soul.

OLIVER

As dawn's light slowly appears in the small room we're standing in; I finally turn to face Chance. His expression is filled with sadness, not pity like I expected, and I'm thankful for that.

"I've never told any submissive I've had in my life that story before. Nathan is the only one who knew." My voice is low, almost a whisper. I don't know why, but my heart aches for him to hold me. But the moment he moves closer, I lift my gaze and lean back—emotions war within me as I continue. "I didn't tell you this because I want you to pity me. And I've never admitted what happened because I never want people to feel sorry for me. If it weren't for that experience, I wouldn't be who I am today. Stronger, more alert, but also, I wouldn't be the man before you."

He nods in understanding, and I know his own experience must've allowed him to face the pain and work through his trauma to come out on the other side. Chance is strong; he's a man with conviction, he fights for what he wants, and I respect that.

Inhaling a deep breath, I watch him for a moment, looking into those green eyes that shine with confidence and pain, with the resolve of what happened to him, and the acceptance of where he is right now. I respect that about him—that he's walked away from something horrific and made a better life for himself.

Doing something I've never thought I ever would, I take Chance's hand in mine. The warmth of his touch scorches me, and I have to suck in a breath to keep from leaning in to kiss him, to hold him. I need to confess how I feel, or at least try to.

"When you told me what happened to you, I was raging inside. There was so much anger I needed to resolve, but nobody I could take it out on. When my men found that asshole, I wanted to rip him to pieces, to slowly slice his flesh from his bones. Perhaps it had something to do with my experience. Maybe not, I don't know."

"I get that," he tells me. "It's something I have felt over the years, and now I know even revenge isn't as soothing as most make it out to be. Yes, the person may have suffered pain, they may even beg for mercy, but you're the one who walks away with blood on your hands."

I nod. He's right. "So wise for a young man." I smile, allowing the tension which filled the room to dissipate somewhat. "Nathan called me, told me about your plans for another one of the Seven Sins clubs," I tell him.

"I wanted to—"

"Where were you thinking of moving to?"

His gaze burns through mine in the dark room. Even though there's only a smidgen of light, I can see his expression clearly. He wasn't expecting me to ask that. Perhaps he wanted to leave because of me, but when I told him I wanted him, I wasn't lying. I've made my choice, and I'm not letting him go so easily.

"I wanted to go back to New York," he finally tells me. "It's where I grew up, and I'm hoping I'm able to make a name for myself in the city my father loved so much."

"And is there a place for one more in your plans?" I step closer to him, needing to feel his warmth. I've never been an affectionate person, and right now, it's no different. I want to fuck him, own him, claim him. Make him realize I'm here, and he's not going anywhere without me.

"Maybe. It depends." He chuckles.

Cocking my head to the side, I smile. "On what?"

"If this overly confident asshole wants to move to New York with me or not," he teases, and I know there's a time and place for everything. But right now, I want him bent over this goddamn desk.

Gripping his arms, I spin us around so he's facing the window and I'm behind him. My hands trail down to his hips, gripping them as I tug him against my cock.

"This is how much I want to move to New York with you," I hiss in his ear.

Chance responds by pushing his ass against the bulge that's prominent in my slacks. The friction against me draws a groan from my chest, vibrating through me, and my need to be inside him is overwhelming.

Working his slacks, I pull them, along with his briefs, down his thighs. With one hand on his back, I push him down until he's bent over the wooden top. His body is mine. Only mine. The possessive force that hits me steals my breath.

"In my bag," he offers, and I know what he means. I unzip the duffel and pull out a small tube. Flicking the lid, I squeeze some out, watching the liquid trail over the cheeks of his ass. Fuck, he's beautiful bent over and willing just for me.

"I want to whip you, Chance," I tell him while I shuffle and tug at my belt, pants, and underwear. "I want to make you fucking groan my name over and over again. Spread yourself for me. It's time I show you just how much I want to own you. Because you're mine, and I will be the one inside you. Nobody else, just me."

Once my cock is released from its confines, I slap it on the lube which shimmers in the yellowish light of the rising sun. The slippery liquid coats my shaft, and I'm jerking myself slowly while my other hand teases the tight ring of muscle, easing Chance open enough to take me balls-deep.

Nudging his opening with the tip of my dick, I move slowly, inching myself into him. Chance is tight, fucking vise-like as I move my hips toward him. Our grunts and groans are the only sound in the room. Testosterone is hanging heavily in the air surrounding us.

"Just fuck me, Oliver, please," he moans in a low, feral growl, and I can't hold back. I slam my hips home, and I'm fully seated inside him. I still for a moment, because I'll come too soon, and I want to savor this moment. I've never claimed any of my submissives before.

Every sub who's been trained by me I've allowed to walk out, to find someone who can offer them the one thing I could never do. But right here is the realization that this moment is where I finally face my demons and admit defeat.

I was always at war with myself. Knowing for a fact I could never love, I didn't. But Chance broke down those walls and made me see that I need to fight for it. Instead of lazing around like a wayward teenager, I need to claim what I want.

A life with him.

"You want this?" I hiss, pulling out and slamming back in, driving him into the desk. His hand moves to his cock, stroking it slowly as I watch his biceps work themselves into a frenzy. The sight of him is too much, and I have to close my eyes. I can't come too soon.

I continue fucking Chance, hard and slow, fast and deep. Our bodies are made to fit together. They're like puzzle pieces that fit perfectly with every groove and dip. My hands grip his hips, holding on as I begin to move faster. I can't hold off my release. My spine tingles with pleasure as Chance's body tightens and pulses. I want more. I need more. Gripping his throat, I pull him up, my fingers curling around his column as I squeeze until I hear his choked pants. His moans are broken and distorted by his lungs attempting to pull in breaths.

His body bows to mine, and as much as he's sucking in tiny gasps of air, his eyes have darkened with violent lust, and the turbulent emotions thundering through me cause my own grunts to echo around us.

My hips slap against his body, my cock plunging balls-deep inside him as I brutally fuck him into the desk. The wall shudders with every thrust, and the paint slowly peels from the concrete as the wood gets shoved against it, again and again, until I feel my release trickling like a river along the rocks. It travels up my spine.

His body convulses around me, and I'm lost. My mind blacks out, and I drive into him, the base of my dick right at his entrance as I fill him with jet after jet of hot release. My body cocoons his. The warmth of us is astounding as our breaths even out.

When I finally slip out of Chance, he turns on wobbly legs to face me. He grips my neck, pulling me in for a kiss. Our lips crash together, our tongues duel and dance, fighting for dominance. It's feral, animalistic. It's everything I ever wanted, but everything I never knew I needed.

For the first time in my life, I'm in love with someone. And he loves me too.

OLIVER

I'm startled awake by my cell phone ringing on the nightstand. My body aches, but there's a delicious tension that's got my cock hard for some early morning sex with Chance before we head out to the home I grew up in. I wanted to show him my past, allow him to walk into the space and see where I came from.

But when I pick up the phone, I notice a number I've avoided calling most of my life.

"What?" I bite out without greeting the man who was meant to be my uncle—the man who hurt me more than I could ever imagine.

"He's gone." The line dies, and I sit in silence for long moments. I don't move. My body is rigid. I don't feel sadness; there's nothing inside me. No pain, no relief. I'm numb.

I don't know how long I'm frozen in place, but Chance shifts on the bed, sitting up beside me, and his hand gently lands on my shoulder. I don't turn to him, not wanting to see the sorrow in his gaze. The same emotion I can't bring myself to feel.

"He's gone," I repeat the words to no one in particular. "My father is dead." As realization sinks in, I close my eyes and try to allow my heart to hurt, to experience the grief, but there's just emptiness.

"I'm sorry, Oliver." Chance's voice drags me from an abyss of nothing, and I meet his green eyes that are peering at me with affection. The emotions that flicker in his eyes dance like a flame; there's a light in them that reminds me of what I'm doing here. They speak volumes, and they offer me more than anything I could ask for — love.

"No need to be sorry." I push off the bed, tugging my underwear up, then my slacks. I shrug on a shirt, buttoning it up.

"Where are you going?"

"To sign the papers, get the house on the market,

and sort out the shit he left me with," I tell the man I love. The man I want in my life forever, but I can't bring myself to utter those words. Not right now. Not in this town.

"I'll come with you."

"No," I snap, immediately hating myself for shutting him out. "I mean, just . . . Give me some time. I need to think." Grabbing my keys and wallet, I leave the room and shut the door behind me. I don't know why I shut down, but deep down, I wonder if it's my pride. I don't want Chance to see a broken man. I want him to love me when I'm strong, when I'm in control.

Shoving my hand into my pocket, I realize I forgot my damn phone. I pivot back to the room. I push through the door only to find Chance getting dressed, his suitcase on the bed, and I realize he's about to leave.

"Don't."

"No, Oliver. You wanted me last night. You showed me pieces of you. I saw all those fragmented shards, all the ugly, the dark, and the broken, and guess what? I accepted you. I agreed that we could work this out. But this morning, you're back to your old self. Cold and rigid."

"My father is dead, Chance."

"Yeah? Well fuck, Oliver, I would never have guessed. I love you and guess what happens when someone loves you? They're meant to be there for you. If you need to cry, do it. If you need to scream, vent, or rage, fucking do it. Just do it *with* me, not without me."

His voice resonates through me, hitting me right in the chest. My heart stills, stutters, then gallops in my rib cage. I open my mouth to speak, but he continues his tirade.

"This is fucking ridiculous. Be the Dominant who fucked me last night. Take charge of your life. You're no longer seventeen, Oliver Michaelson, you're a fucking grown man, and all I want to do is fucking submit my everything to you. Can't you see that?"

"Come with me."

"What?" His eyes glimmer with unshed tears. I've never seen so much pain on someone's face before. Never seen heartbreak right in front of me, but with Chance, I don't just see it, I feel it.

"You want to be there," I tell him. "Come with me.

Stand beside me as I lay my father to rest. I don't know if that's what he would want, or perhaps he'd want his ashes spread across all the whorehouses he frequented." My tone lowers when I realize I didn't know much about my father at all. I never took the time to ask Dad what his last wish was, and he never allowed me close enough to care. I almost made that same mistake with Chance, pushing him away. I almost lost the best thing that's happened to me. "I guess, whatever I do" — I shrug meeting his gaze — "I want you there."

We stand there, face to face, at a standoff.

"No more closing yourself off."

"I promise," I tell him. "Now get your ass in my car so we can go."

A small smile plays on his lips, and I know he's happy as the emotion shimmers in his eyes. He's a commanding dominant at times when it comes to women. But when he submits to me—making my cock stand at attention—I can't deny, it's one of the hottest things I've ever seen in my life. And I want it forever.

In the car, I question, "So, you want to submit to me?" I risk a glance his way, waiting for him to take back what he spewed in the room. Perhaps I'm expecting him to say it was said in anger or frustration, but he shocks me with his response.

"Yes. I want to be yours. Like I said to you in the house a few nights ago, I'll be everything you need, Oliver. Even with your training, I want that life. We're cut from the same cloth. We need a third person for the excitement of it, but I know in my heart, I love only you."

"We'll talk," I tell him as we pull up outside the small office where my uncle is leaning against the window, smoking a cigarette. I'm not ready for this, but if I don't do it now, I'll never be able to face it.

The funeral is tomorrow. There's nothing more for me in this small town. Recalling my past was painful, but I know I couldn't have done it without Chance beside me.

The clouds are pulling over, darkening the sky, and as I watch the sun disappear, I realize with affection how in his own way my father pushed me to be better. At sixteen I was lazy, young, and stupid. I didn't want to live in a big city. I didn't even want to go to school. All the times he made me get up in the morning, I hated him. The never-ending jeers from classmates, even from teachers, forced me to focus. It's only now he's gone that I realize all he did wasn't because he hated me; it was because he wanted a better life for me.

Turning, I watch as Chance pulls the suitcase I packed from my old room down the hallway of my childhood home. I have work in the city, so we need to head back to Chicago. The city where I found my happiness.

Big green eyes meet mine for a second before they turn away. He hefts a heavy case into the trunk and then another. Once he's done, he ventures inside to find me. I've been standing at the window for so long I've lost track of time.

"Are you ready?"

Nodding, I meet Chance's curious gaze. "I am. I was just saying goodbye to memories," I tell him before following him out and shutting the door behind me. Soon, the house will be sold, and I'll donate the money to charity. It's finally time for me to put the past behind me and focus on work. My undercover business has been busy these past few months, and with every new job that comes in, I know I'm helping those who need it.

"This is the last time you'll ever be in this town," Chance tells me. "Are you okay with that?" His gaze meets mine, reminding me why I left here in the first place. He is the reason I'll never want to come back here.

"I've never been more at ease with my life." Reaching for his hand, I pull it into my lap, lacing my fingers through his. "It's been a long time since I have let anyone in, and you have given me something I never knew would be possible, Chance."

"Let's go home."

Nodding, I turn the key, starting up the engine, and pull out onto the road. It will be a long drive, but I'm looking forward to clearing my mind of the past while I drive toward my future. Almost twenty-six years ago, I left this town behind, and now I'm leaving it once more. Only this time, I won't be returning.

CHANCE

I've never done road trips, but sitting beside Oliver for eight-and-a-half hours has been interesting. We spoke, more so than ever before. His favorite color is black, his choice of city destinations would be London, and he loves Scotch. There are so many more things we learned about each other, and even now, as we pull into the driveway of his home, I can't help but smile. I took Cayleigh's advice, allowed myself to be honest with him, and it paid off.

Granted, there were many instances where I was ready to walk out. And I think he's realized he does indeed love me. Even though he's not said it yet, I know it will come when the time is right. It's not something I would force on him. Yes, it would be wonderful to hear him say it, but it needs to come from his heart.

When he pulled into a small motel last night, we got some sleep, but it was restless. The remaining drive back to Oliver's house, I've been sneaking glances at him. He's let me in, and it's a strange feeling watching a man so strong — so confident — hurt so much.

I can't believe I broke through his high barriers and I found the man who'd been hidden away for so long. As soon as the engine dies, I cast another glance his way, and I know this is where I'm meant to be.

I've made the right choice.

For once, I've chosen love, and it's paid off.

I want to be here — home with him. I can't wait to get inside and offer him everything I've been holding back. I want him to give me his worst. To let all his pain out on me so we can move forward.

We exit the car, grabbing my duffel and Oliver's suitcase from the trunk. Once inside, we head for the living room where he pours us both a drink. Exhaustion hits just then, and I realize we haven't slept properly in two nights.

There was too much tension and uncertainty. Oliver

hands me a tumbler, raising his own, as he clinks it against mine.

"It's time we moved on from our pasts. I'm not an easy man, Chance, and I can't promise you I'll ever be easy to put up with, but if you're willing to give this a go, I'll be right by your side."

I can't help but smile. It's been a rollercoaster, that's for sure. But then again, no relationship is perfect from the get-go. We all have to overcome trials to find the happiness we all strive toward.

"Oliver, I don't expect you to be perfect, or even saintly," I chuckle.

"No chance of that happening."

I rise to full height, so we're face to face. "There's nothing wrong with letting me in." My words are a whisper, filled with tension, desire, and hunger. I want him to give me everything he has. "Take me to the playroom. Lose yourself in me."

"Are you sure?"

Nodding, I gulp my drink, setting the glass down on the table. "Yes." I meet his gaze. "I want it. Show me."

He quickly swallows his Scotch, and we head down

the hallway toward the door that holds his secrets. Once we step inside, I take note that nothing has moved or changed in any way since the last time we were in here.

"Take off your clothes," he orders from behind me. The deep tone of his voice sends warmth coursing through my veins. I rid myself of my shirt and slacks. My socks follow, and then my briefs. Once I'm completely naked, I meet his stormy gaze.

"How would you like me?"

"I want you on the bench, kneeling." His husky tone is evidence he's already turned on.

My cock jolts at the thought of being bound on the spanking bench. I make my way over to the piece of furniture and kneel on the stirrups. Oliver moves around me, binding my wrists with the cuffs and my ankles with the thick leather straps.

He doesn't speak when he blindfolds me. The touch of his fingers is so gentle, and I know it's a stark contrast to what I'm about to experience. My ears prick as I hear the shuffle of his clothes, the clank of his belt buckle, and the soft *whoosh* of whatever he has just picked up.

"What are your safe words?"

"Red and yellow," I whisper into the darkness. I'm trembling with need. I want him to touch me, to stroke my hard cock, to do something to me, but I'm met with nothing. The silence is so thick it's deafening.

Suddenly, the whoosh of air and the sting of what I'm guessing is a crop, licks against my flesh. A moan escapes my lips, tumbling into the room. Another bite, another sting, and I'm tense in attempting to hold back the orgasm that's tightening in my gut.

"Is this what you wanted?" Oliver's voice is right at my ear, the heat of his breath feathering over my skin making the hair on my neck stand up.

"More." My husky murmur is clear. The room is heavy with sexual tension. Oliver moves toward me, crouching so we're face to face.

"You're not the one in control," he tells me. Then, he rises, and another lick against my flesh causes a grunt of pleasure to vibrate through me. Another one lands on my ass, and my toes curl.

His one free hand grips the cheek of my ass, squeezing, making my cock jolt with pained pleasure. My balls are tight, ready to empty, but Oliver steps back, giving me space to come down from the edge.

"I want to mark every part of you, Chance."

The crop falls to the ground with a skitter. Then, another sound flies through the darkness, and I'm swatted with a flogger. He's moving the pain up a notch, and I cry out as pleasure and pain slams into me—my cock throbs. My balls are heavy, ready to explode.

"Do it, please. I need it. I need you." My pleas are turning low. The vibration of the sounds of pleasure rockets through me, and I'm on the precipice.

"If you come, I'll cane you." His words drip desire.

Another harsh swat on my ass causes me to moan out loud. "Oliver, please?" I call his name, begging for release. My eyes are shut even behind the blindfold. I see white sparking behind my lids, my attempt at holding onto my impending release is a slowly losing battle.

"Are you sure you want to be mine?"

The lick of leather wretches another plea from me. More and more, he whips me, causing my cock to throb. I bite my bottom lip until I taste blood as I'm so hard. So fucking ready to fuck him, to slide into his tight body.

I feel his heated breath on my cheek, then his tongue

laps at me, licking the tears that have streaked past the blindfold. His tongue teases my mouth, licking the crimson, and I know he's savoring it.

I've watched how his steel gaze turns stormy when he's turned on, and I can only picture how those beautiful orbs would shine with a blizzard of desire. And the need to see them now grips my chest, my heart, and I know there's no longer a way I can walk away from him. I love him. This is it. Forever.

"So, fucking delicious. Now I think you may have earned your orgasm." He rises, leaving me trembling, and I close my eyes beneath the blindfold to keep my release from coming too soon.

A snap that echoes through the room causes me to groan as hunger tightens my stomach, the need seemingly turning to a storm about to hit. A moment later, the cold liquid he dribbles on my ass is my salvation. It eases the welts I know are rising, and it taunts my hole, readying me for his cock. His fingers move slowly over the welted skin, his touch scorching me into an inferno of lust and sin.

He eases one digit into me slowly, pumping in and

out, then a second enters me as I focus on the way he's finger-fucking me. Oliver works me into another heated frenzy, and I'm once more begging him, pleading with him to show me mercy.

Oliver doesn't respond. His control over my body, over my orgasm, is the only thing he's focused on, and it makes every nerve in my body spark with electricity.

Gently, he eases out of me, the emptiness making my body alert. This is it. I need him inside me. "Sir. Oliver, I need you, please."

"Once we take this step, it's final," he speaks as he teases me. The tip of his cock right at my entrance. The heat of him, the way I tighten, pulsing for him to finally enter me.

"I'm yours." It's a promise. One I will never break.

The way my body is shaking, he knows I'm barely holding on. Oliver sinks into me. The movement is slow, methodical, and I know it's about to explode through every part of me.

His cock inches into my tightness, throbbing as he feels me tighten, pulsing around him. His hands grip my hips so tight I know I'll be bruised, but I don't care. All I need is him fucking me into oblivion, claiming me as his.

He pulls out, then inches back in. The movement is slow and torturous, and I'm tugging at my restraints. I want to fuck myself back onto his cock, but he knows I'm unable to move.

Once he's fully seated, he stills for a moment, and I'm whimpering like a fucking kitten. "Oliver, please, fucking own me. Please."

And he does. Pulling out almost all the way, he slams back into me, causing my brain to short circuit, and my toes curl as pleasure ripples through every inch of my body. He's fucking me so deep I feel his heavy balls against me. The sound of skin slapping, of grunts and groans, are all that echo around us.

I'm lost to him. Only him.

He spanks me hard on the welts he marred me with. Again, and again. The sting of pain and the bite of pleasure. They all culminate in a moment as his one hand grips my shaft, tugging me, jerking me off, and his low growl in my ear, "Come for me," sets me off, and my orgasm tears through me like a hurricane named Oliver.

I feel his heat fill me while I paint his hand with

white fluid, and I know we've both just marked each other for life. There's no longer a reason to leave. It's forever, and nothing can change that.

OLIVER

"You're awake early," Chance says from behind me, but I don't turn to face him. I keep my gaze on the coffee maker. Last night was something else. Something inside me clicked, and I knew there was no way I would ever be able to walk away from him.

You'll never make anything of yourself. My father's words come loud and clear. Usually, they'd hurt, slice through me, but this time, they don't. I'm happy for the first time in a long while, and I know nothing can break me down again.

Smiling, I turn around, meeting his green eyes. He doesn't move, as if he's waiting on me to confess my feelings finally.

I nod. "All my life, I've been scared. I realize that

was what held me back for so long. I didn't want the pain of seeing someone I love to walk away or leave me. Trust wasn't something I allowed myself to offer, because each time I did let myself give into that emotion, it was broken, shattered, and I couldn't go through it again."

"That's why you needed the lifestyle," Chance says. "Training the submissives, you had the control over who left and who stayed." I nod in agreement. "And then I came along."

"Well, you and Cayleigh rid me of everything I'd been hiding. But even though I cared for our sweet Irish princess, I knew she was meant for other things. And that's where you came in," I tell him, setting the mug of now steaming hot coffee on the countertop.

"Oh?"

I nod. "It's time to lay to rest the demons of the past." Picking up my mug, I inhale the scent of mocha. The coffee is dark, the scent thick in the air. "I realize I've been just like my father for so long I turned into the man I hated all my life. And it's time that stops."

"What does that mean for us?" As always, Chance cuts right through the bullshit and asks just what he wants to know. He looks deep into the parts of me I have kept hidden for so long. It's time to unlock the box and show someone the real Oliver Michaelson. Maybe it's time to finally confess what it is I really do with the business I run secretly.

"If I tell you—"

"I'm not going anywhere," he insists, which makes me smile. There's fire dancing in his eyes. The confidence in which he utters those words gives me a glimmer of hope that perhaps he's right. Maybe not everyone leaves.

"I know you're not. I started a business not long after I got my degree. At first, it was just following around assholes cheating on their wives. Over the years, as that paid off, the client base grew. There were so many people out there that needed help." Picking up my mug, I drink down the coffee, allowing the burn of the liquid on my tongue.

"And you found your clients at Seven Sins?" His question catches me off guard. I wasn't expecting it, and I'm unsure of how to proceed. I simply nod. I suppose it's time to lay it all down on the counter and allow Chance to make up his mind.

"Yes, they knew they could trust me. I'd been frequenting Sins for a year. Their friends who also met me through the club trusted me. And so, Michaelson Investigations was born. Even though it's an undercover operation, I still enjoy law, so, I focus now on training new law students and allow them to work at my company while they're studying for the bar. And most of the women in my office know about my Dominant side, and that's why I have them there."

He watches me for a moment, processing my words. Then, the moment I think he's going to tell me this is not going to work for him, he nods. "So, your office is filled with subs who allow you to train them?" His brow arches, and I nod.

"Yes. It's not a sexual thing for me. I am offering them a job, with the benefit of becoming submissive for someone. To learn and explore the lifestyle without getting into a relationship with some asshole who could hurt them."

When I hired the first girl years ago, I wasn't sure if it was a good idea to mix business and pleasure, but over time, it's become something I look forward to. And it's true, my scenes at the office aren't about sex. They're about punishment and reward. Teaching the ladies who are there, and who want it, to live the life twenty-four seven.

"How is it, after all you've been through, you find the warmth in your heart to help others? To teach, to make sure they're safe and cared for?" Chance muses while sipping his hot drink.

"I don't know. I suppose, seeing others live through pain or heartache, it doesn't sit well with me. Over time, I knew I could make a difference, and I focused my energy on that. Yes, there were times I lived in the past, I held onto everything I'd been through, and I allowed it to make me as fucked up like my father."

"But you're not like him, that's my point. You may see yourself like that, but Oliver, you're nothing like the man who couldn't even support his own son." Chance rises. Stalking around the breakfast bar, he stops right beside me. His green eyes shine with affection as he regards me.

"It's difficult for anyone to see past what others may deem faults, whether it's skin color, sexual orientation, or even weight and height. Society pushes us into molds. If you don't fit into whatever the rest of the world deems *normal,* then you're the outcast."

Chance's gaze meets mine in realization. He understands what I'm trying to say, what I've always believed. "And you end up believing it."

"Yes, you believe the lie, and you live by it." I agree. "People are so hellbent on all being the same, when it's the uniqueness of the individual that makes you who you are."

"When did you become so wise?" Chance teases, a smile cracking on his handsome face, and I can't help but chuckle.

"When I hit forty," I retort playfully. It's foreign to me, to feel so at ease with someone, but with him, I do. Leaning in, I plant my lips on his. A soft, gentle kiss that causes him to groan ever so slightly, but I hear it. Our bodies press against each other, the need running rampant through my veins.

I dart my tongue along his lips, requesting him to open to me. To allow me in. And he does. His tongue dances with mine, licking along the muscle, sucking it into his mouth. His teeth graze along it, which elicits a rumble from low in my throat.

I'm hard, but I need to get to work. *Fuck.* When I pull away, his stare is glassy, and pupils dilated with desire.

"Tonight. You and me," I inform him, then, as I lean in closer, inhaling his spicy cologne, I finally admit just what I've wanted to say before the moment he walked out of my house a few nights ago. "I love you, Chance Moore."

EPILOGUE

CHANCE

SIX MONTHS LATER

My sister smiles up at me when I enter the house. I haven't been back since Oliver and I decided on making our relationship official.

"Love looks good on you," she states, planting a soft kiss on my cheek.

I eye her from head to toe, noticing how beautiful my sister looks. She's glowing, and I know for a fact, it has to do with the tiny bump she's sporting. "And kids look good on you, apparently?"

"Funny . . . Carrick says the same thing." She winks playfully, causing me to shudder at the thought of my sister's sex life. It really isn't something I need to be thinking about.

"Please, my mind is a happy place without that visual." Chuckling, I follow her into the kitchen where a pot is steaming on the stove. The scent of something delicious is coming from the oven, and I'm sure dinner will be amazing. I recall when I was younger, our mother would teach Peyton everything she knew in the kitchen. When our parents died, we were lost for a long time before finding our path in life.

"So," Peyton starts, and I know the torrent of questions is about to start. "You and Oliver . . ." Her words taper off. She's fishing for information, but there's not much to say. Yes, we're together. Yes, we're planning a wedding of sorts, and now that he's teaching me the dominant side, I'm looking forward to my new life as a switch.

All my life, I had a clear path of who I wanted, what I wanted, and then Oliver Michaelson walked in — no, sauntered in — and I was a lost cause. With him, I'm submissive, giving him everything he needs, but with the women who kneel for me, I'm Dominant in every way.

"Say what you want to, Peyton," I tell her with a smile on my face.

She stops stirring the pot and turns to me. "I'm happy for you. I mean it, Chance." She grins. "There's nothing more I want than to see my brother happy. And Oliver does that. He gives you what you need, and that's all that matters."

I'm about to respond when the deep rumble of the man I love sounds from behind me, and the footsteps of him and Rick cause me to turn around.

"I heard my name." Oliver reaches Peyton and lifts her hand with his, pressing a kiss to her knuckles. "It never seems to stop, women and men talking about how amazing I am."

"I think you need to get taken down a notch there, Michaelson," Rick offers with a laugh. My brother-in-law grips my shoulder, offering it a squeeze in greeting. "Chance."

"How are you, Rick?"

"Good. I was about to take your man here to the office so we can finish up a few contracts before lunch."

Peyton sighs at her husband, rolling her eyes as she questions, "Are you working on a holiday when I asked you not to?"

"Listen, little lady." Carrick moves closer to his wife. Gripping her hips in his hands, he tugs her toward him. "I'll be done in a few minutes. You're catching up with Chance anyway." He kisses her, and I see it, the love that surrounds them. It's like an entity, and I know deep down my sister finally has happiness. It's taken years for her to find it, but I pray to all that's holy she'll never let it go.

"Mommy!" A screech comes from beside me, and I notice one of my nieces racing into the kitchen with an empty bowl. "My ice cream is finished."

"And just where did you get ice cream before your dinner?" Erin's cheeks turn bright red, then her big green eyes that match my sister's fall on her dad's. "Did you give the girls dessert?"

"It was a snack." Rick turns his attention to Oliver. "Let's head to the office." He doesn't wait for Peyton to respond, and I can't help laughing once we're alone.

"He's insufferable," she mumbles, taking the bowl

from her daughter. "Say hello to Uncle Chance."

The little girl, who's not so little anymore, runs my way to hug me, wrapping me in her slender arms. "Hi, Uncle Chance."

"Hi, Erin. Where's your sister?"

"She's playing," she tells me with a toothy smile, and I wonder if I'll ever have the opportunity to be a father. "I go outside." Then she turns to her mom. "'Kay, mommy?"

"Yes, just don't get in the pool. Dinner will be ready soon."

"Okay!" she shouts and races out of the kitchen. Peyton looks incredible. Her skin is glowing, her hair is loose, hanging in waves down her back, and her stomach is slowly swelling with a baby boy. They found out only a couple of weeks ago.

"So," I start, leaning on my elbows on the kitchen counter, watching my sister. "I was wondering if you'd be my maid of honor?"

The spoon she's holding clatters to the plate as she spins on her heel. Her mouth falls open, gaping at the question like a fish. I want to chuckle, but I know she's in as much shock as I was when Oliver told me we're going to figure this out.

He may not be a relationship type of guy, but our agreement has come to an end, and we're not parting ways. We came to the conclusion that we enjoy what we do. The training, the scenes, and the club — they all culminate in our pleasure. The fact that Oliver wants me wholeheartedly but still wants to train submissives is perfect. I want to Dominate them, but I want nothing more than to kneel for him as well. To serve and pleasure him any way I can.

"Are you telling me you've tamed the beast?" Peyton grins, her eyes twinkling as she questions me.

"Tamed wouldn't be what I'd call it. More like, encouraged." Her brows shoot up, then furrow in confusion. "We're together. Like, getting married, but . . ." I didn't realize how nervous I would be admitting what our life would be like. At first, it sounded perfect, but telling someone else about what we like is nerve-wracking. Granted, I doubt my sister would judge me, but I've lived with people's judgments all my life.

"Well?"

"We'll be training submissives together. Oliver enjoys dominating me, and I enjoy dominating women, so, we've come to the conclusion that it works for us. We love each other, but we both need more." Lowering my gaze, I don't want to see her reaction. The fear of her telling me it's bullshit rears its ugly head, and I wait for it.

"Hey." Peyton steps up to me, her hand on my cheek. "This is beautiful. Life and love, they're amazing when you have someone who can love you so wholly they want you," she tells me. "If this is what you both need and both agree to, then nobody can judge you for how you live your life. I'm happy for you, brother."

"Really?"

"Of course," she laughs. "As long as you're fulfilled and Oliver takes care of you. If he doesn't, I'll kill him."

"You're a feisty little thing." Oliver guffaws from the doorway as he enters the kitchen with Carrick close behind.

"You don't know the half of it," Rick agrees, pulling his wife into his arms as he places a kiss on her forehead. "She can be scary, I assure you of that."

"So, what do you say, Peyton?"

A smile lights up her face. "Yes, of course, I'll be your maid of honor, silly!" The girls come racing into the room, both begging for juice and candy, to which my sister tells them it's dinner time.

We make our way into the dining room and settle in our seats. With a glance around the room, I can't help smile at the happiness that emanates from me. This is my family with the love of my life. This is what dreams are made of.

Cayleigh

Smiling up at the clear blue sky, I bask in the sunshine that heats my skin. The splash of water nearby reminds me of where I am, and I can't help but be happy. Something clicked inside me the moment I stepped off the plane at LAX. I can't explain it, but I felt as if I have a new start at a life I've always wanted.

"Hey!" The screech makes me giggle. Nate and Eva's kids are sweet, and even though I've never spent too long with children, I enjoy watching them bicker and twist their dad around their little fingers. Nathan is a commanding force, reminding me of Oliver, but as soon as his daughter and son are at his side, he softens and gives them the love they need.

My phone vibrates on the table beside me, and when I pick it up, I feel the blush heating my cheeks. Desire tightens in my belly, and I'm off the lounger in seconds.

When I reach my bedroom, I shut the door and lock it. Hitting dial on the number, I press the phone to my ear. Within three rings, his deep, commanding tone filters through.

"Hello, kitten," he greets me in his thick Italian accent. Everything about the man I met at Sins two weeks ago has got me hooked. Tall, dark, and handsome, his tone is gentle, but there's an underlying current of dominance that causes me to squeeze my thighs together.

"Hello, Matteo." I smile at the way his name rolls off my tongue. Flopping on the bed, I lie on my stomach, legs bent at the knee, and my feet in the air.

"I have some business to take care of this evening, but I'd love to see you afterward," he tells me. Even though we've only been seeing each other for a couple of weeks, I'm excited by the prospect of more.

Smiling, I respond, "Yes, I'll be at Sins helping Eva with the event." Tonight, we're having a masked evening, where every person will be in black and white, along with the masks that were sent to members.

"I know." His answer makes me laugh. "You forget, *gattina*," he murmurs. "I know everything there is to know about you."

"That's what I get for dating a mafia prince," I retort playfully, causing a dark chuckle to ripple through the speaker, making my heart leap wildly. Matteo Moretti is Mason's cousin. Mason and Carrick own Seven Sins in Chicago, and the ties to the Italian mafia on Mason's side are strong.

When I learned the connection to Savannah's husband, I told her. I think Mason and Carrick may have had a chat with Matteo, and even though my brother would've possibly threatened Matteo, he hasn't shown any sign of relenting in his pursuit of me.

"I'll find you this evening on the balcony," he tells me in a hushed whisper, and I wonder if he's in a meeting. At times, he'll call me while in meetings with his brothers, Franco and Gio.

"My dress will be—"

"Don't tell me, *gattina,*" he tells me. "I will find you. You know I like to play hide and seek, and when I find you, kitten . . ." His words trail off into nothing; the silence is the promise. My nipples harden and my panties are wet from thinking about what he's going to do to me.

"I look forward to it, *il sicario,*" I tease him, calling him a killer because I know he's done bad things, and each time I utter the nickname, he only chuckles.

"*Ciao,*" he says before hanging up.

Rolling over onto my back, I stare stupidly at the ceiling with a grin on my face. My new life is turning out to be everything I need to start fresh.

Oliver

The office is empty.

Everyone has gone home, and I'm sitting back,

staring out at the city slowly coming alive as the moon hangs in the dark sky. Chance told me not to be home before seven, so, for the first time in a long while, I'm obeying him instead of the other way around.

Glancing at my watch, I notice it's almost time to leave. He thinks I don't know what he's doing, setting up dinner, preparing a special meal for us. The thing is, he doesn't realize I have a gift for him.

I should've been the one at home, setting the table, making sure the food is ready as soon as he walked in. And when he enters, I would be sitting with a tumbler waiting on him to gift him the item I bought.

Instead, he has been fighting me tooth and nail to cook, so I allowed him that one privilege to mess with my plans. With both of us enjoying dominance, there are times we have a push and pull, and even though it would've annoyed me in the past, with Chance, I bask in it.

Grabbing my jacket and keys, along with my phone and wallet, I head out of my office and down to the garage. When I slip into the driver's seat, my phone pings with a message.

I don't read it.

I don't need to because I know it's him.

The ride home doesn't take me long. And when I finally pull into the drive, I notice none of the lights on. Frowning, I exit the vehicle and head inside. The foyer is silent. There's not a sound coming from the kitchen, which is rather strange.

But the moment I step into the dining room area, I see him. Chance is standing at the windows that overlook the backyard. He's dressed in a dark pair of slacks, and a shirt that looks white, but with the candlelit room, I can't be sure.

"I'm guessing dinner is ready?" I question when I near him, taking in the place settings. The china is expensive, a set I bought so long ago I'd forgotten I own it.

"It is." He turns. Smiling at me, he hands me a glass with a shot of alcohol. A smoky fragrance comes from it, and I realize it's my favorite malt whisky.

"This is rather fancy," I say, waving my hand over the table. Two candles sit in the center, the flames dancing in the darkness, making Chance's skin flicker with the glow.

"It's a special evening," he tells me, and my heart leaps into my throat.

If he means what I think he does, I may want to take him upstairs and fuck him into next week. Stepping closer to him, I swallow my drink, savoring the burn for a moment before reaching my hand around the back of his neck. I pull him toward me, our lips inches apart.

"Tell me," I command. My tone is husky, needy for him to admit what I already know. We've been talking about this for months. And with the wedding coming up, I plan to focus solely on the dream he has of running a club in New York once we're married.

Chance clears his throat, a small grin playing on his lips. "Carrick and Mason signed off on my business plan. I'll be the proud owner of the NYC club."

Pulling him in, I press a kiss to his lips. "And I'll be right beside you."

"Are you sure you want to leave Chicago?" he questions, and I knew this is something we would need to discuss.

"My job can be done from anywhere in the world,"

I tell him. "And being beside you is the only thing that matters. Now, I have something for you." Stepping back, I head into the foyer and grab the gift box that was delivered yesterday. The moment I saw it, I knew it would be perfect for Chance.

When I return to the dining room, I place the box in his hand, waiting for him to realize what it is. The click of the lid echoes around us, and those green eyes I've been losing myself in for the past few months lift to mine, and the wetness that shines in them makes me smile.

"This . . ." He lifts the object from the black velvet. A sleek silver band which will fit around his wrist perfectly has an onyx stone in the middle. The engraving on the inside is something I had personalized just for Chance. "This is . . ."

"It's yours. It means you're mine. I wanted to give you a collar, but this is something I'd love to see on your arm forever."

"But the wedding—"

"The wedding is for our family. This is for us," I confirm. It's true; this is our private moment, only for our eyes.

"I love you, Oliver. You are everything to me."

"And you're my world." I smile. "Forever."

Have you read the rest of the series?

Kneel (Book #1)

Obey (Book #2)

Indulge (Book #3)

Ruthless (Book #4)

Bound (Book #5)

Envy (Book #6)

Vice (Book #7)

Acknowledgments

Reaching the end of this series is bittersweet. Yes, I'm going to miss these characters who've spent the last couple of years with me, but I'm also excited to move onto something new.

This may not be the last time you see them, but this will be the last story in the Sins of Seven Series. Thank you for loving these couples, for your support and reviews, and for taking the time out of your busy schedules to message me about them.

Thank you to my BETA's—Allyson and Cat—you ladies are amazing. I don't know how I could do this without you!

Candy, my editor, your hard work on my manuscripts are pure magic. Thank you for everything!

A huge thanks to my my Angels street team—Tre, Sheena, Sarah, Lisa, Caroline, TJ, Hayfaah, Joy, Cinders, Kathy, Sara, Tanya—thank you for pimping my work EVERYWHERE. You ladies rock!!

My reader group, The Darklings, as always, you're the only place I know I'll find like-minded ladies and a handful of gents who will have a laugh without drama. The group has grown so much and I'm excited for the future! Thank you for being there.

To all my author colleagues, thank you for always sharing, commenting, and supporting me. I appreciate every one of you. Having a support system is important and you ladies provide that and so much more.

Readers and bloggers, from the bottom of my little black heart, THANK YOU. All you do for us authors is incredible. Reading and reviewing is demanding on your own time and you do it with a smile. Thank you so, so much. You are valued and appreciated for taking time out to show us so much love.

If you enjoyed this story, please consider leaving a review. I'd love you forever. (Even though I already do!)

ABOUT DANI

Dani is a USA Today Bestselling Author of dark and deviant romance with a seductive edge.

Originally from Cape Town, South Africa, she now lives in the UK with her better half who does all the cooking while she writes all the words.

When she's not writing, she can be found binge-watching the latest TV series, or working on graphic design either for herself, or other indie authors. She enjoys reading books about handsome villains and feisty heroines, mostly dark, always seductive, and sometimes depraved.

She has a healthy addiction to tattoos, coffee, and ice cream

www.danirene.com
info@danirene.com

FIND DANI ONLINE

Do you follow me?

If not, head over to any of the below links,

I love to hear from my readers!

Amazon - http://bit.ly/DaniAmazon

BookBub - http://bit.ly/DaniBookBub

Facebook - http://bit.ly/DaniFBPage

Facebook Group - Dani's Deviants

Goodreads - http://bit.ly/DaniGoodreads

Twitter - @danireneauthor

Pinterest - @danireneauthor

Instagram - @danireneauthor

Spotify - http://bit.ly/DaniSpotify

OTHER BOOKS

Stand Alones

Choosing the Hart

Love Beyond Words

Cuffed

Fragile Innocence

Perfectly Flawed

Black Light: Obsessed

Among Ash and Ember

Within Me (Limited Time)

Cursed in Love (collaboration with Cora Kenborn)

Beautifully Brutal (Soldati di Sangue)

How the Mind Breaks

The Devil's Plaything

While She Sleeps (Dirty Heroes Collection)

It's Never Easy (Lady Boss Press)

Only One Night (Lady Boss Press)

Deviant (Black Mountain Academy)

Taboo Novellas

Sunshine and the Stalker (collab. with K Webster)

His Temptation

Austin's Christmas Shortcake

Crime and Punishment (Newsletter Exclusive)

Tempting Grayson

Gilded Sovereign Series

Cruel War (Book #1)

Volatile Love (Book #2)

Sins of Seven Series

Kneel (Book #1)

Obey (Book #2)

Indulge (Book #3)

Ruthless (Book #4)

Bound (Book #5)

Envy (Book #6)

Vice (Book #7)

The Taken Series

Stolen

Severed

Four Fathers Series

Kingston

Four Sons Series

Brock

Carina Press Novellas

Pierced Ink

Madd Ink

Broken Series

Broken by Desire

Shattered by Love

The Backstage Series

Callum

Liam

Ryan

Forbidden Series

From the Ashes - A Prequel

Crave (Book #1)

Covet (Book #2)

Printed by Amazon Italia Logistica S.r.l.
Torrazza Piemonte (TO), Italy

38486558R00194